Willesden Herald
New Short Stories 9

www.pretendgenius.com

Published simultaneously in the United States and Great Britain in 2016
by Pretend Genius Press

This compilation copyright © Pretend Genius Press 2016
Editors: Katy Darby, Stephen Moran

ISBN 978-0-9852133-7-4

Willesden Herald

New Short Stories 9

Pretend Genius Press

Foreword

Many thanks to Katy Darby for judging the Willesden Herald international short story competition 2016.

The stories are in the sequence in which they were originally read. Their layouts have been replicated as far as practicable. Some have initial paragraphs of sections indented, some don't; some have single quotes, some double, some none; section break styles vary etc.

If you enjoy these short stories, as I'm sure you will, remember there are plenty more in the back issues! Thanks for reading.

Stephen Moran
www.newshortstories.com

Introduction

It's a rare and wonderful thing to read a short story that truly excites you. It's even rarer and more wonderful when that short story is by someone you've never heard of. I hope that every reader of this book will feel something kindle in the pit of their stomach at least once as they plunge into these stories. It may not happen when they read the winner, or even one of my own personal favourites: but if Steve Moran and I have chosen right – and I believe we have – it will happen. And it will be wonderful.

In the last ten years, since co-founding the live fiction event Liars' League, and starting to teach creative writing at City, University of London, I've published a respectable number of my own short stories, and one novel – but I have read literally thousands of them, classic and modern, published and unpublished. Yet I still get a thrill when I come across one which has all the right ingredients: style, pace, insight, wit, intelligence, feeling, a unique way with words, and that *je ne sais quoi* which means you will remember it long after less well-crafted stories are forgotten.

Most of the stories it's excited me to read have been unpublished, because there's a unique thrill to discovering a new story or author for the first time: for the moment, at least, they are your special secret. The only thing better, in fact, than discovering these gems is sharing them with others – which is what the New Short Stories anthology series, and the international fiction competition that created it, have been doing ever since the tireless Steve Moran set it up in 2005.

Several of the stories in the book I fell in love with at first sight – the title alone hooked me, in some cases, making me eager to turn the first page – but some revealed their true quality only on a second or third reading. Some, like *The Mayes County Christmas Gun Festival* by David Lewis, are here because they made me laugh – and because there aren't (and probably never will be) enough stories out there which are just as funny as they are clever; both whip-smart and witty. Others, like Anna Lewis's thoughtful and bittersweet *The Volcano* drew me effortlessly into their world; the characters were subtly drawn and ins-tantly credible, and the depth and heft of the story was worthy of a novel. Then there were the shorter pieces, like Gina Challen's haunting *Undercurrents*, which mesmerised and amazed me in equal measure: how did the author cram such a richly textured narrative into such a small space? How did she manage to say so much with so few words?

The best of these stories, though – and in my view, the best *kind* of story – is what the musical theatre industry would call the "triple threat". In the world of the West End, the triple threat is a performer who can act, dance *and* sing. In the world of fiction, for me at least, it's a story which can make a reader respond intellectually, emotionally *and* viscerally: and I believe this year's first prize story is a superb example of this (literally) winning combination.

Critics are often accused of cliché when they praise a book because it made them laugh and cry – yet in the end, don't most of us read to be moved, whether to laughter, anger, wonder or tears? My favourite stories are those that make me think *and* feel; these are the ones that make me giddy, and get me excited. I hope the ten stories you're about to read have the same effect on you.

Katy Darby
Prize Judge 2016

www.katydarby.com / @katydarbywriter
www.liarsleague.com / @liarsleague

The Volcano

Anna Lewis

My pen hangs loosely in my fingers as I run over in my mind the opening to the letter. *William, it has been far too long. Please forgive me for my silence. You were the first person ever to show belief in my silly little poems...* I don't like the letter's tone. It is, as I always have been towards William, too grateful and too humble.

But the words are true. It was twenty years ago, but his face leaning towards me across the little wooden table in the Square of the Martyrs is still the image I see when I think of him, and still the image I see when I think of poetry. Lamps were lit around the edges of the square, and a fat candle spluttered on our table. Although the air was beginning to cool, it remained rich with the smell of roast onions and garlic and meat; small groups talked rapidly at every table around us, and from the church on the northern corner of the square bells began to sound. The lights of an aeroplane passed, slowly and noiselessly, far above.

I was a country boy – I still am, but an old one now – and I was in awe of everything around me. The square seemed like some ancient quarter of Paris or Rome, with coloured lightbulbs strung across the faces of the inns and boys droning their scooters over the cobbles, girls clinging to their narrow waists. Later that night, William said in his strange, drawn-out accent, the vowels long and the consonants swallowed, "It's unbelievably quaint, this town. Like something out of a fairytale."

I looked again at the cobbles and the lightbulbs and the candles on the tables, and saw that we were not in Paris. A shade darker than the sky, the bowl of hills rose up behind the rooftops. I thought about the modern plaza, beyond the cobbled alleys which surrounded the Square of the Martyrs, where the buses terminated and where twice an hour you could catch the train to the airport. That was not Paris, either.

"Do you know my poems?" William asked me, his eyes and cheeks hollow in the candle-light. I didn't: I couldn't read a word of English.

"Well, I suppose you write yourself?"

I did, but was not published. I had travelled to the city that evening because I loved to read, and because I was excited by the idea of hearing so many famous authors deliver their work. Now the readings were over, the authors and the audiences were eating and drinking in the square, and everyone seemed to know each other. The tall, light-haired man who joined me at my table, without asking, was one of very few other people who appeared to be alone.

"May I see your poems? Do you have any with you? Here." He leaned over and filled my empty wine glass from his own carafe. I was embarrassed and flattered. I had a handful of typed-up poems folded together in my briefcase, and I handed them across the table. He frowned and sniffed as he read them, occasionally taking a large swallow of wine. After a few minutes he looked up and said, "Interesting... very interesting."

I had not been drinking while he scrutinised my papers, but now I gulped, and coughed.

"You write in formal metres... these are traditional forms?"

"Yes – in those poems there are a couple of different forms. It's all to do with the internal rhyme scheme and the pattern of the consonants, as well as the syllable-count – they are very old metres..."

He nodded. Straightening his back, he said, "I work in the modernist vein, myself – I like to play around with form, break it apart and put it back together, you know? I could have some fun with these poems. Would you mind? If I were to have a go at translating a couple, fooling around a bit?"

I was amazed. The wine he had poured into my glass was revolting, but even that did not detract from the huge question of his face beyond the candle. "Of course not," I said, "Keep them, keep them."

"Wonderful." He folded the papers into quarters, and squashed them into his jacket pocket. He motioned towards my wine glass, and I pushed it towards him over the table.

He took my address, and although I had half forgotten about our encounter, I thought of him immediately when six months later I found a package on my doormat bearing a row of American stamps. His name was on the reverse, and what I took to be a university address. Inside the package was a journal of poetry, printed on coarse paper and with a lurid red cover. On page 28, underneath his name, was a sentence in smaller print which included my own name, and beneath that was the text of three poems. The form of the poems was unrecognisable: my even lines were fractured and split, sometimes to just one word, and at other times stretched to the width of the page. But with an English dictionary I translated the titles, and saw which of my poems was which: *Spring; My Mother; Snowdrops*. I have always liked my titles to be simple, and those were some of the earliest poems I had written. Later I would write other poems about spring, and other poems about my mother. In my new manuscript there is a poem about that first appearance in print of my poetry, and I have called it *My Mother in the Spring with Snowdrops*. I wonder whether William will notice the reference.

That magazine is still propped on the shelf above my desk, others beside it. William sent me a note, tucked inside that first journal, thanking me for my poems and asking me if I had any others. Half in excitement and half in panic, I sent him all the decent poems I had. I heard nothing more for almost a year, and then another magazine arrived, printed on glossier paper. Inside, underneath William's name, were translations of half a dozen of my poems. *The Mountain; The Well; Sleep...*

I showed the magazine to a colleague of mine at the school, who spoke good English. He looked back and forth between the shiny pages and the crumpled sheets on which my original poems were typed. "Some of the vocabulary is the same," he concluded, "But the grammar, the syntax – it's all broken down. And the form is gone – there's no metre."

I said, doubtfully, "I think that's what he told me he wanted to do. But do they make any sense? Are they... ugly?"

"I don't really understand poetry," my colleague said, with a shrug. "There are bits that make sense and bits that don't." He held out the magazine and my papers, and I had to steady my hands to take them. "Congratulations, though!" he added. "Look at it! You're published in America. You're famous."

I was not famous, but a gleam of excitement remained. In the time it had taken William to translate and publish nine of my poems, I had succeeded in publishing only one myself, in a regional poetry newsletter. I had torn the page from the newsletter, mounted it in a simple frame and hung it in my hallway, but everyone who entered the house commented on it, so I took it down. My father-in-law asked me each time I saw him – at least twice a week – "And how is the poetry going? Any more success?"

"Nothing, nothing," I always said, "But I'm writing."

My father-in-law struck me between the shoulder-blades with his enormous hand. "Of course you are! That's the way!"

I sent William more poems, and he sent me translations in print. More magazines, and clusters of poems in anthologies. In one of the anthologies, another American poet included translations of Rimbaud, and another translations of Miłosz. My name was in the same book. My wife kissed me when I showed her, bouncing on the soles of her feet.

William sent me another letter, not constructed as painstakingly as usual. Although he spoke naturally, his written language was stilted and usually over-precise, but his latest note was scattered with mistakes. Words were crossed out here and there, the ink was smudged: his happiness and urgency was clearer in the mess of the letter than in anything he actually said. A large publisher in America had commissioned a volume of selected poems, in which the best from all of his earlier books would be republished together. *This is a good walk for me. I am moving from a small publisher to a big publisher, I am from a small poet to be a big poet.* Translations of three of my poems would be included in the book, and there would be a small royalty for me.

A year later the book arrived, and soon afterwards another letter, once again carefully composed. *There have been reviews in many newspapers and magazines, all of which are positive – apparently, my book is good! Several reviewers have commented on your poems, which are a source of interest and wonder. Happily, I will soon return to Europe, to speak at various educational and cultural establishments.* A month or so later came a postcard from Hamburg. *Some spare time after my tour. I would like very much to visit again the country of my parents, and if possible I visit you in your home. Send me your e-mail? We have so much to talking.*

I could not imagine William at our home, in our tiny village in the mountains, a four-hour drive from the capital. If he had thought the capital quaint, what would he make of the world beyond it? The roads were even worse than they had been when he was last in the country, and I had heard that the train from the airport into the plaza now ran only once an hour. I stared from the kitchen window over the valley. On the far side the school was hidden in mist, as was the stone bridge that connected the main village to our hamlet. I could see nothing but the bank of trees below, and the corner of my neighbour's yard. His two dogs circled each other in the muck.

From behind me, my wife reached her arms loosely around my neck. "Come on," she said, "He wants to see what it's really like, doesn't he, the place his parents came from?"

"Who says they're from here? They were from down south somewhere, I think, and now he's been being wined and dined all over Europe. We can't do anything for him."

She dropped her arms to my waist. "It's not a case of doing anything for him – he's an old friend of yours. Besides, I bet he'll like it here – he's the sort."

I would have done anything to please her, then, although I think she believed that she was pleasing me. I was curious to see William, but I was ashamed of my dishevelled country, my dirty village, my old-fashioned cottage and, for the first time, of my job, which I had always thought responsible. But really, what did it consist of? I taught peasant children to read and to do sums. Most of them, like their parents, would do nothing but stay in the village all their lives half-heartedly working the fields; otherwise they would traipse to the city to break their backs in factories or on building sites. If they could be bothered they might read the newspapers, they might one day vote, but there was nobody of any worth to vote for. William, meanwhile, had spent the last two months roaming across Europe, speaking at various educational and cultural establishments.

But no matter. William, the internationally-renowned author, liked my poems. In his hands my poems had become a source of interest and wonder; and it was true that we were, in our way, old friends. On the afternoon that he was due to arrive I stood at the end of the stone bridge in bright sunlight, my wife beside me with her arm linked into mine, and felt a tremor of hope. At the top of the valley, above the school, the white stone of the church sparkled, and I could just hear the tumble of its bells. Below us, the river cut a shapely path to the south.

"This one, maybe." My wife clutched at my arm as we both caught the rumble of an engine on the air, and we turned together as a red car passed into view beneath us. It disappeared again almost instantly into the trees, but emerged onto the final bend a moment later. No one in the village owned a red car. I lifted my hand in greeting before the car was close enough for me to make out the passengers; as it drew level, then stopped, I felt my smile spread. The passenger door opened and a tall, thin figure unfolded from the seat. My wife's hand slipped from my elbow as the long arms wrapped around me, let me go, then wrapped around me once again.

"My dear friend!" When he let me go the second

time we were both laughing. My wife, standing to the side, was smiling too, with her hand over her mouth.

The tour had been magnificent. For someone, he said, who had been a nobody for so long – a young nobody and then, far worse, an old nobody – he could scarcely believe how kindly he had been treated. His photograph had been in city newspapers, he had been put up in marvellous hotels, and crowds had come to see him read. Many students, and many others too. He had met so many poets. So how was my own poetry going? He reached across the table and clapped my hand in both of his. "What have you published? Show me!"

My hand felt small as a child's. I pushed back my chair and walked unevenly to my study, where from among the magazines and anthologies William had sent me I flushed out the couple of newsletters and two thin magazines in which my own original poems had appeared. "Not quite an output to rival yours," I said, handing them over my wife's head.

He looked at the covers and front pages of each before turning to find my poems. "Interesting," he said. "You see, this country lacks... it doesn't have a proper publishing infrastructure. What are these, local papers? University magazines, that kind of thing? It's good, it's fine, but you need serious publishers too."

"There are serious publishers," I said. I was still standing behind my wife and couldn't see her face. "Poetry is serious business here. But none of them are interested in my poems."

"Well, I don't believe it." He cast through the papers briefly and tossed them down. "I'll read your poems properly later, if you'll let me. But I don't believe it."

My wife motioned towards the pot in the centre of the table. "Would you like any more, William?"

"Thank you." He helped himself, and began to talk again, through mouthfuls of casserole. "I haven't tasted food like this since my childhood. Restaurants in the capital, they all serve Italian, French, and none of it good. Why is that, tell me? This is the food of the nation."

"Your mother used to cook this kind of thing?" my wife asked.

He shook his head, chewing. I took my seat once more. "Not my mother. We all used to eat together after church on Sunday, in the community hall. I grew up in New Jersey – are you familiar with New Jersey?"

"In New York?"

"Close enough. You know how it was – you know how few people got out of here, after the war. But half of those who did ended up living on a few blocks in New Jersey. They opened a church and a hall. I had to go to Sunday school. We spoke the language at home, of course, but at Sunday school they tried to teach us to read and write it. My god, it was boring! And all that dusty peasant art on the wall. My parents were sophisticates, you know. Like yourselves. But the Sunday dinners... I was a skinny kid, you know. I ate nothing all week because all I could think of was the Sunday dinner. I'll dream of it tonight."

My wife motioned towards the pot again. Her cheeks were slightly flushed, her lips parted in a small smile. She had the same look, sometimes, when we had dinner with other couples we knew and talk turned to their children. She would ask questions, tilt her head as though to hear the answers all the better, but she never offered any comment. She would let them talk and talk. On the steep walk home back up the side of the valley, our breaths in the air above us and the wine we had consumed muffling us against the cold, she might say suddenly, "That boy sounds a terror," or, "I don't envy them their middle one." But that was all.

"Thank you, but I'd burst."

My wife shared out the last scrapings from the pot between her plate and mine. After coffee, William said that he was ready for bed. We had made up a couch for him in the spare room, and through the wall we heard the springs squeak and the blankets rustle, then the floorboards groan: first at the far side of the room, then the near side, then the far side once again.

"What is he doing?" my wife whispered.

I didn't know. We had drunk a lot, the ceiling was shifting above my head; and whatever William was doing now, I was not concerned.

A strong rain fell through the night, and although by morning it had lessened to drizzle, mist filled the valley. Rather than walk all the way to the main village in the damp and cold, I led William around the hamlet, and along the edges of the surrounding fields. Here there were enough tumble-down cottages and pigsties and chicken coops to satisfy him. Two small girls in tracksuit bottoms and tee-shirts passed us on the other side of the lane. "Good morning, sir," they said in unison, aiming identical suspicious glances at William.

"Good morning, girls," I replied. "Don't catch cold, now."

"No, sir." They took turns to look back over their shoulders as they went on.

"You must know all the children here," said William.

"I've taught most of their parents, too. The

generations shuffle along quickly in a place like this."

"Oh, I daresay."

We walked slowly up towards the centre of the hamlet, where the two lanes crossed, and turned right onto the intersecting lane. Now we were on the path which skirted the field behind our house, although a broad lynchet at the top of the field prevented sight of it. The cloud was thickening again; before us, the lane was dim.

"It broke my parents' hearts, leaving, you know," said William, turning to look at me directly. "They never spoke about the old country, hardly ever told me anything. I had to learn about the war from books, you know. Encyclopaedias at school. And they refused to go back, and then after the uprising they were too old. Things were too volatile, anyhow. But it broke their hearts."

"It must have," I said. I couldn't think of anything to add. I couldn't imagine New Jersey at all.

"It's one reason why I love your poems so much," he said, his voice deeper and confidential. "Your poems are a link to their world, the world they left, and to my own past, you know? When I translate them, it allows me a way in – to the war, to the uprising, the displacement – it's there in my hands, in your words and in my words, do you know what I mean? I should *thank* you, is what I'm saying, I suppose."

He spoke so swiftly, in his odd accent, that I wasn't sure if I was following him. "But I don't write about the war," I said, "Do I? I've never written about the uprising."

"The three poems of yours that are in my *Selected* – which are they? – *Sleep, Sunflowers, My Mother...*"

"None of those are about the war, nothing like that –"

"But to me – to me – they speak of it. The sorrow, the dislocation, times lost... it's all buried in there. I take your poems apart and I find it, I carry it out. It's the beauty of your poems." He let his hand rest on my back for a moment. "You're the real thing, my friend. That's why you can't see it."

Later, warmed and comforted by lunch, I tried once again to make myself understood. "The thing is," I began, "It's just that... I was born after the war. We both were. And my parents never spoke about it much either. I wouldn't write about it, I wouldn't know how. But the uprising – your parents weren't here for that, but I was. I remember it – it took a big chunk of my childhood."

I looked across the table at my wife. She nodded.

I went on. "It wrecked the health of both of my parents. They both half-starved, making sure my sister and I had enough to eat. I didn't understand at the time, but I realised later. It was like that for everyone here. You say that leaving broke your parents' hearts, but staying and living through the uprising – it broke my parents' spirits, it damaged their bodies. I don't want to be melodramatic."

"My friend, you could never be melodramatic. That's what I *mean*, that's what I'm saying to you. The pain in your poetry is subtle – everything is implied, it's all metaphor. You're not writing about these things, and you are, at the same time."

"But I'm *not*. What I mean – what *I* mean – is that one day I might want to write about the uprising. I don't know. But when I do, it will be my way, my memories."

"You need to understand where the interest lies in your own work! Or maybe you don't. Maybe your very naivety gives it power. But little rhyming pieces in some esoteric, dusty metre – poems about flowers and birds and oh-so-sad, oh-my-poor-mother – people don't need them. Not in America. When I hold up your poems and show people the war, the uprising, the – the trajectory of my parents' exile out of their land and *out of their own lives* – people see the profundity. They feel it with their hearts and they understand."

My wife stood up. "It's a long drive back in this weather," she said. "I think we had better call the taxi now." I still remember the way he looked between us, from her face to mine, and back. I saw that my wife met his gaze. I let mine fall.

My father-in-law brought us a bottle of cherry vodka for our wedding anniversary, bound with a golden bow. "Quite the thing, down south," he said, and when my wife went to place it on the side, he pulled it back out of her hand. "Open it, share it! Who brought you up?"

My wife, laughing, tugged it back from him and waved it at me. "Take it! It will all be gone in five minutes!"

"And why not?" I took the bottle from my wife, handed it back to my father-in-law, and strode into the kitchen to look for glasses.

"How is the poetry?" he shouted after me.

"I'm still writing."

"What's that?"

"I'm still writing!"

And I was, but nothing was published. Here a scrap, there a scrap. The editor of the regional newsletter had retired at the new year. He posted me a card, thanking me for my charming contributions. I can see the corner of it, pink, poking from the shelf above my desk.

For a long time after William's visit, he sent no

more word. I sent him no more poems. I rarely mentioned him, and neither did my wife. Then I saw in the newspaper that he had received a major award, a prize that would surely guarantee him fame beyond his own lifetime. The article made much of his heritage, and said that although he wrote mainly in English, he translated occasional poems from his mother-tongue. *His mother's tongue*, I thought. *Not his.*

My sister telephoned me from the south. "You're famous!" she announced through static. "Well, you're not. That's what you're famous for."

"What are you talking about?"

"You know your American? The kids looked him up on the internet, and found an article from some American magazine – about you!"

"About me?"

"Yes, but the thing is, it doesn't think you're real. It's so funny, the kids translated it to me and I don't know how to explain it. Shall I send it to you?"

"I don't understand what you're talking about, seriously – "

"I'll e-mail it to you."

I printed out the article from the computer in the school staffroom, and handed it to my colleague. He stood leaning against the back of a chair, lit a cigarette, and smoked studiously as he read. Ash trickled down onto the carpet. The school day was over, the children and other teachers had gone, and dusk was heavy across the playground. I put out my hand to the radiator, which retained only the slightest warmth.

"Essentially... essentially, the author admires the poems that your American has translated. I mean, he admires your poems. But he casts doubt on your identity. He says that in your own country you appear to be unknown. You have published no books. He points out that you have no internet presence. He is suggesting that you are your American's alter-ego – an artistic fabrication."

"What's that?" my father-in-law shouted into the kitchen.

"I'm an artistic fabrication!"

There was a letter from William. He was so sorry that he had been out of touch for so long. Our hospitality had been marvellous, but he had the feeling that the visit had ended on an awkward note. He deeply hoped that this was in his imagination. At any rate, he was booked onto a lecture and reading tour of the United Kingdom, in connection with the little prize that he had unaccountably been awarded (perhaps I had heard?). In April he would be attending a festival of translation in London, and as he would be speaking partly about his translations of my poems, would I have any interest in joining him there? My expenses would all be covered. We would each read, we would have a conversation and open it to the audience; we would, perhaps, be able to air some of the points we had touched upon during his visit to my beautiful home.

For a few days I tried not to consider it, but through my head the Thames flowed steadily on, the lights of Big Ben and the Houses of Parliament reflected like stars. I saw cyclists and joggers gliding along the Embankment, a cool, sunlit morning, the trees all in bud. And I saw William: the face that had leant towards me on the Square of the Martyrs now caught in a gentle spotlight, while below us rows of other faces lifted silently.

There was, I started to think, so much to say. So much to say to William, so much to say to all those people who would be there at the festival regardless, who would hear William's translations but who knew nothing, really, about my country, nothing about our history and the way we write. And there were my new poems. The manuscript, pinched together by bulldog clips, stood at the end of my bookshelf: all the poems I had written since William's visit, none of which I had sent to him. My poems were changing; the old forms still clung to me, but I moved differently as I carried them, pulling them in new directions. They were malleable now: they had grown to trust me. I wanted to stand up and speak the new poems aloud, and I wanted to show them to William.

"You have to go," my wife said. We had left the shutters open so that we could look out on the snow while we ate, and so we were both cold, bundled in woollens at the table. The walls of our neighbour's farmyard were obscured. His ancient dog was chained to the side of the outhouse, and sat howling; the sound seemed to come from very far away. "You'll always be hankering after it if you don't go, dreaming of what it might have been like."

"It might not be a bad thing to make up with William, I know. He has been good to me."

"It's been good for him to be good to you. But yes."

"It's not just William I'm thinking about, though. You'll be in hospital. Why does it have to be at exactly the same time?"

"Look, it's a routine operation. My father can pick me up afterwards – it will be fine."

Just as my parents never discussed the uprising, just as William's parents never discussed the war, my wife and I never spoke about the blight on our own marriage. After my wife's second miscarriage, both almost at full term, we had agreed not to try for more children until we felt we could both bear more disappointment. Neither of us had raised the subject again. I had the impression, from television and films, that Americans talked all the time, never stopped shovelling up the contents of their souls. I was glad not to live like that; but we had to discuss the operation, we had to make plans.

As snow fell more thickly against the window, we agreed that we would travel to the city together and spend the night at a hotel there, which would allow us both to be ready early in the morning. I would accompany my wife to the hospital, ensure that she was booked in and that there were no last-minute complications, then I would catch the train to the capital. My flight was due to leave in the late afternoon. By then, I hoped, my wife's operation would be complete and she would have woken from the anaesthetic. If not, I would not hear from her until I touched down in London.

"I do want you to go," she said. "I just hope I'm not still under at the same time as you're flying. We'll both be in unnatural states. I don't like the idea of that."

"We'll just have to see," I said. "The plane will probably be late, anyway."

"My operation will probably be late."

"True."

Two days before the day of my flight, and the day of my wife's operation, a clerk from the airline telephoned me. I didn't understand what he was telling me until I watched the news.

"Is there no chance it will improve?" my wife asked.

"How should I know?"

I travelled with her to the city and checked in with her to the hotel. We both slept badly, but I held her in my arms all night, the way I had when we were first married. At the hospital she was booked in easily, and shown through a pair of heavy swing doors to a separate waiting area in the gynaecological department. I was not allowed to join her. I kissed her and put my arms around her again, but she pushed me off, embarrassed.

"Go on! We're not teenagers." There was a tear in the corner of her eye which I wanted to brush away, but she was backing through the doors.

"You'll be fine," I said. "I'll be here when you come round."

Feeling half-drunk with tiredness, I returned to the hotel, and ordered a coffee and a pastry at the bar. I sat on an imitation leather chair and watched the news on a large television screen hung between two windows. Through the windows, the early sun shone down on tower-blocks the colour of cinders. The television was muted; sub-titles ran along the bottom of the screen. A trunk of white steam twisted against a pure blue sky. *For the third day in a row, almost all flights to, from and within Europe have been cancelled, as the ash cloud generated by the eruption of Icelandic volcano Eyjafjallajökull continues to pollute the atmosphere.* I ate my pastry, drank half of my coffee, and took myself back to the room. I tried to sleep.

At two o'clock I sat up, brushed my teeth, and walked back to the hospital through gentle spring sunlight. Even in the ugly streets of the city there was blossom on the trees. I sat in the public waiting room on the row of chairs closest to the swing doors. "It's all right," she had said last night, in bed. "The operation doesn't make a difference. It's far too late anyway." I held her tighter. I couldn't think of anything to say.

My nieces and nephews in the south had, it seemed, made a hobby out of searching for me on the internet. William's appearance at the translation festival had been a great success. My absence – my sister chuckled down the line as she told me – had added more fuel to the theory that I was the result of William's imagination. According to one journalist, an audience member had asked William "to general mirth" whether I did indeed exist, "a question to which the poet responded with a silent, knowing smile".

In the weeks after my wife's operation, she was not herself. She was physically weak, which we had both expected, and spent some days in bed, but even as her body recovered she remained quiet and withdrawn. I walked with her around the village, up and down the streets we had both known all our lives: across the stone bridge, around the square, up the walled lane to the school. "I'm not sad," she said, looking ahead as we walked, "It isn't that."

"No?"

"No. I just don't feel like I'm really here. I'm sorry. It will get better."

"I know it will."

Another publisher returned my manuscript, with a note of polite regret. If my wife had been well, perhaps I would have asked her advice. But as the sun grew stronger, as the leaves in the woods grew denser and midsummer approached, I found myself in a constant state of something close to panic. Time was running out. I could not sleep. One morning at the end of May, a short time after dawn, I sat up in bed and then, checking that my wife was still asleep, walked softly to the study. I sat down at my desk and typed a letter. I printed it off and slid it into an envelope, together with my manuscript. I let myself out of the house and, in the hazy light of early morning, walked down to the stone bridge. The river underneath was misty. I pushed the envelope into the letterbox at the end of the bridge before I could change my mind.

By the time the school year ended my wife was noticeably better, although still prone to quiet moods and tiredness. We agreed to take a holiday together, although the operation had eaten into our savings; but it had been a miserable spring for us both. We travelled to the lakes, in the west, and rented a small cabin beside a shingle beach. It was cheap; local fishermen brought their catch around in a cart every morning and sold us the freshest, most flavoursome fish either of us had ever tasted. Once in a while we drank vodka at the café in the village a couple of miles along the shore. The buildings there were all wooden, painted shades of blue and green, and a hut on the jetty hired out pedalos. A faint, not unbearable stink of rotting vegetation rose from the lake and wound through the narrow village streets. We stayed there for a month.

When we returned home, a letter was waiting with a return address in the capital. It was from the university press. While my wife was unpacking I locked myself in the bathroom and sat down on the edge of the bath. I opened the letter beneath the whining fan.

The collaborations are highly interesting... the experimentation with form at once technically proficient and sensitive to the concerns of modernism. The manuscript was *a brave venture* and, after all, *a publication in the poet's mother-tongue is an exciting prospect.* The publishers would be happy to draw up a contract, provided that both William and I would sign. *One last small point: as a title,*

"Eyjafjallajökull" could be difficult to market. Might "The Volcano" be an acceptable alternative?

"What's the matter?" my wife asked me over supper. "We've only just got home. You look as though the weight of the world is on your shoulders."

"Term will start in a few days, that's all – I'm just thinking about it. Sorry."

"It will be fine. It always is."

"I know." There was not a weight on me so much as a colour all around me, and I couldn't tell yet if it was light or dark. "I know. I think I might be looking forward to it."

After a poor night's sleep, I rise soon after dawn. My wife is breathing deeply, rhythmically. There is a chill to the air. I wrap my dressing gown around me before I sit, then take out a writing pad, and set down my address and the date. Automatically, as it always does when I am sitting here, my head tilts back and my eyes pass across the shelf above my desk: the American magazines, the anthologies, William's *Selected Poems*; the first poem of my own I ever had published, cut out from the newsletter and still in its frame, propped sideways among the books and journals. There, the pink corner of the editor's card.

A tardy owl hoots somewhere in the valley. I try not to think too clearly. I try to remember the sound of the lake lifting and falling on the shingle outside our cabin.

I grip my pen. *William, it has been far too long. Please forgive me for my silence. You were the first person ever to show belief in my silly little poems...*

Catherine McNamara

The Cliffs of Bandiagara

Awoman, her son, a man and a trader drive north to Mali to interview a musician for an English record company. The woman is a freelance journalist, the man a photographer. She does not know that the musician is sick and leaving for a concert in Denmark in a matter of days. The interview has been arranged or half-arranged by a man in London whose French is not good, who thinks he has spoken to the right person in Bamako. This is pre-internet, pre-kidnappings, pre-terror videos. The Twin Towers have fallen weeks ago. The land is flat and soundless with her history manifest in adobe mosques crumbling along the ancient slave routes, and painted *Boulangerie* signs in villages where commendable baguettes are sold. The road is a silver spear. The days are dense contracts between these four people.

Between the messy, unscripted towns there are baobabs. Once, the boy makes them stop the car on the side of the road. The engine tickers. The boy has a new front tooth that has come down crooked, which his mother intends to have fixed. The boy leaps onto the dust and declares he is running to the tree, the *bow-oh-bab* tree, that one there, and he begins to elbow the dry air and his sneakers produce orange puffs. The woman had known there would be moments with the boy.

'Let him go,' the man says, stretching his legs and focusing his camera on the tree's distant barrel and arms. The man comes from a coastal West African city; he has been her lover for five months.

The boy grows smaller and smaller, a white wafting on the scrub, almost bodiless. The woman watches. The boy once popped his tongue into her mouth but she knows it was a copied act. Because it pleased her, this mix of animal and man, she told no one. She wonders, when her son turns back to the group by the jeep, what compulsion he might feel towards her: small, braless, wearing a short disrespectful blue T-shirt. Will he recall this scene when he is a man, staring back at some woman he loves?

The trader who is named Cissé remains in the car. He is dressed in a clean white shift and cradles his head. At least once a day Cissé claims he has malaria.

Cissé has them stop at a town he says he knows well. It is Sikasso; they have just driven for miles and miles over rucks of sand. He says they should first buy their baguettes *ici*, pointing to a stall where a girl lies on her arm asleep. The photographer does not like to follow Cissé's recommendations. He is not convinced that the trader needed to come along and dislikes the singsong of Cissé's French. Instead the woman, who once lived in Paris, sees the irony of perfect baguettes under her arm and greasy notes with a northern figurehead flattened on the counter. She hoists herself back into the jeep and gives a heel of bread to the boy.

Cissé leads them to a place where he says there is excellent sheep meat. They are installed in a hot back room on benches and given four bottles of Coke that sit in pools. The green walls are smeared with hand prints to shoulder height. The prints are vigorous; they set off a frequency on the air.

A platter of mutton bones piled high is served by a man in a filthy shirt.

In the town the blond boy is chased by other children and his flat hair is touched. He begs Cissé to tell him how to say *Don't touch me. Please.* Cissé, who is a vulgar man, more vulgar than his companions know, tells him to repeat this in the local language: *My mother, she is horny.*

*

In the morning a dog attacks Cissé on his way back from the mosque. The reddish animal lunges out from behind a shed, sinking canines into his tendons and tearing the surface flesh. It is just dawn and the sellers are out on the road. A busty girl comes up and he does not understand her dialect so they speak in French. Cissé is petrified; his temples are wet. The girl shoos away the growling dog and brings Cissé to her room where she raises his torn ankle and pours over warm salted water, then stinging alcohol. She is young and her kindness makes Cissé wish for his wife. He hobbles back to the hotel where the others are asleep. He walks through the compound. He asks a woman bent over sweeping for some tea but the woman scowls.

Inside the room the boy lies in a netted cot that is just longer than his outstretched body. He sleeps on his back, motionless. The couple have made love in the dark of morning and now lie in repose. The photographer awakens. He covers their bodies and stares up into the netting. He wants to put his fingers inside of the woman next to him but he does not want her consciousness alive or her body animated. He lies still. His cock is soft and he cups it in his hand. There was a woman from his city a few years ago who had fallen pregnant with his child. It happened just when his love had begun to burn. Each day he had photographed every region of her body. Her manly shoulders and short, humpy breasts; the knuckles of her spine as she crouched to wash her sex, fingering herself as she squatted. But the young woman came home one afternoon and said she'd had an abortion. Said they were living in a bubble. She left him for an American journalist who was later shot. What he was told was this: the man had arranged an interview with an opposition leader in a neighbouring country and drove up to the politician's house. A police officer put his pistol through the window and discharged.

If he concentrates, he can still cry for her. He used to believe that the photographs of her body were his most intimate images, but his work has improved and now he sees that his obsession made her hidden to him, and these photos were bereft of craft. In one, she has a white cloth knotted around her neck. She has a boxy forehead and she turns away, her body twists; she stands before a half-built house on the salt flats out of town. It was not the story he had seen or wished to tell, but it had emerged. He has learnt that much of his work is subterranean, that he must lie in wait. Recently, he was told that she has given birth to a daughter.

The singer his new girlfriend is to interview was groomed by one of the icons of Malian music, a man who lived for decades within the embrace of the West. At sixty, he grew tired of concerts in Bercy and the clucking of people and the breasts of white women. He dreamt of irrigating the barren fields around his village with channelled well water; he heard the sound of gushing water in all moments. The old man severed his record contract and returned home to his wives, and his absence left a vacuum that was filled by the young disciple. This man, in the music world, quickly became known for his immense talent and rudeness. Many journalists, given fraudulent directions, have failed to negotiate the dusty warren of Bamako's back streets.

*

After breakfast she leads him to the shower recess where a trickle falls over their necks. He rises to her, they grapple and laugh, he pierces her and knows the shower taps are grazing her back but she likes the pain, he has seen this. He dislikes her biting; he prefers fluid lovemaking. The child watches them return to the room half-dressed. She tells him to brush his teeth. He is disgusted that the child enters the bathroom where they have just fucked, then his disgust separates from him. *It's her child.* His children will never be subjected to this. In fact their affair is instructing him how to correct his life in advance. Looking ahead, he suspects they will last a few more months before the sex is spent and the boy becomes paramount to her. When the boy goes out into the sunlight, he savages her lips.

Outside they see the boy is speaking with a man on a bicycle wearing a wooden mask. The mask is elongated, chalky white with sea-blue dots; inverted triangular incisions for eyes and two hare ears curling forward. Standing astride the bicycle, the man holds the mask to his face, tilting down to the boy's captivation. He talks in muffled phrases. The woman paces over to the man who can only be a seller. She does not know that the cyclist is the brother of the busty girl who bathed Cissé's ankle that morning. Cissé, by way of thanks, had told the girl he was travelling with a white woman when he saw a pile of artefacts on the floor. He had given her the name of the hotel.

'You want buy? *Tu veux acheter?*' the hare man is saying to the boy.

His mother cups his shoulders, pulls him back. The large-headed man frightens her with his turbulent voice. Cissé watches from a stool in an alcove. The photographer thinks that perhaps there is a shot if the woman and child would move away. The hare man on a bicycle as a mythical outlaw. He sees that his woman is braless, accessible; she has told him she can be no other way. Now he sees Cissé staring at her small evident breasts. The hotel manager flies out and chases the cyclist back onto the street.

The woman drives. They reach the outskirts of the town and head forth along a sealed road into the scrub. There are less baobabs and fewer ruins in this area, and they have brought bottles of bright orange Fanta and grilled peanuts in newspaper cones. After an hour she stops the car on the side of the road. There is waist-high grass and she goes off to pee, unzipping her jeans as she walks away from the jeep. She is gone a while and her lover grows edgy, thinking of snakes. He looks out but she has crouched down and he can't see her. It is not concern that he feels, but exasperation with her flights. She emerges from the grass calling his name, tells him to bring his camera. Leads him away into the shrill column she has made through the plants. At a distance from the car she pulls off her T-shirt and throws herself down in the grass, topless in her jeans.

'Photograph me,' she says. 'Photograph me.'

He catches her arms on the scratchy pressed halo, her plum nipples and the contortions of her face. Her skin is a shimmering, colourless garment. He brings her torso into focus, thinking of her organs overlapping in shades of dark red. She wants him to straddle her but he will not. She pulls him to her and their faces are bitter.

In the car the boy empties a Fanta bottle, hands it to Cissé who throws it wide into the grass. The boy asks Cissé why he wears a dress like a woman.

*

Bamako rises like a defeated cloud before them. The heat repels them, traffic tosses them to and fro. Cissé who lived here as an adolescent tells him to swing right, *No swing left! À gauche! Ici!* The photographer drives now, his lover is solemn at the window and the boy asleep. Scant directions were sent by the London office but Cissé says they are all wrong, says that the musician she is to interview lives at the opposite end of town from where they are headed. The photographer mentions the quartier of his colleague Sami, married to a French air hostess, where they have been invited to stay. Cissé's hands fly out again – *à gauche! à gauche!* – and it is clear that he is clueless. The woman rolls her eyes. Cissé finally sits back, smiling out the window at the stream of bars and dwindled Pan-African monuments along the thoroughfares. The boy wakes, climbs over the front seat, curls into his mother's arms.

*

Sami's house is a low cool bungalow with concrete support struts throughout the main room. The front veranda has been screened off and writhes with contented plants. They are seated out here. Sami's house-girl serves them duty-free Pastis from France before bringing out a round of local beer. Cissé's hands agitate between his legs. He drinks a bottle of Sprite. The photographer knows Sami from a major exhibition, held here, where both of their images were praised. Sami runs a small gallery which he would like to support. The woman feels her lover is distant from her now, even inconsiderate; she sees he is relieved to be in fresh company. He laughs hard at Sami's jokes. He asks of Sami's wife, the French air hostess Kitty, who is doing the Dubai-Paris-Rio route this week.

She takes her son to the bathroom so she can look through the house.

She sees the couple are childless. She sees that Kitty has a deep love of traders' beads which are coiled on tables; that she collects the indigo-stained cloth they weave here; that she admires the blocky Dogon horsemen who ride across their porous constellations. There is a framed photo of a European woman with a fringe that brushes the top of her sunglasses. There are prints of Sami's work on the walls. They are tight, sharp portraits of Malians. She wonders if Kitty is fleshy and broad and giving, a vivid juxtaposition to Sami's work. She wonders how it would be to spend most of the day in the air, groundless.

Her son is hungry. In the kitchen she asks the young girl for *une banane*, absurdly happy she has produced a riff of French without thought. Her son peels the banana and eats it. The girl's hand drifts over his blond straight hair. The boy says the words Cissé told him and her hand jerks back.

In the evening a woman named Maryam comes to Sami's house. She is a local singer and she knows the musician the journalist has come to interview. She knows him well. She knows his compound; it is on the outskirts of Bamako and it is very difficult to find. But she will show them. Do they know he has a concert in Denmark this week?

Maryam's hair is shaped into two majestic eaves that entwine at the back of her head. The small boy wants to touch these elaborate, necking snakes. He kneels on the couch beside her, his clear hands reaching through the air. Maryam arches her neck in his direction.

The photographer has spent the afternoon speaking of his current project with Sami. It is a political project with an Algerian colleague, which will document the offspring of the generals executed during the coup in his country. Now, he is fascinated by the tilting of Maryam's body. The asymmetry of her face and shoulders and one breast below the other, its form compressed. He wants to study the itinerary of Maryam's movements. He feels a transaction is already in place. He feels this sense of transaction with the best of his subjects.

Maryam sang last night until the early hours in a low-ceilinged bar in central Bamako where she has followers. Maryam is tired of speech, though she enjoys the white starfish of the boy's hands straying over her neck and upper arms, they are cool.

When Kitty is abroad Maryam stays with Sami. Her hair lotion and face cream and brassières and lacy thongs are in a locked cabinet in the maid's room. A few dresses are at the back of the house-girl's wardrobe. Maryam wants to make love with Sami before her body falls to the earth and her throat is gripped by a dark hand. Sami's tongue will render her blind and lifeless. Maryam lifts herself. She walks barefoot to Sami's bedroom and closes the door.

Sami's gardener has taken their bags from the jeep and placed them at the foot of a double bed in a converted garage along the side of the property. The room is narrow and a ceiling fan makes low swoops. Sami announces that Kitty's brother is an anthropologist, Philippe, working in the north, and they should disregard *ses affaires*. When Sami bids them goodnight the woman tugs off her clothes and walks naked to the attached outhouse, where her lover hears the smattering of water on tiles. She does not call him. He and the boy look at each other. The boy stares into his eyes in the absorbent way of children. The man lies out on the bed.

The boy throws his pillow to the floor. He curls on top of the sheets and turns to the wall.

When the woman comes out still dripping the man is dreaming: he has seen her vanish into blades of grass;

he has left the metallic vehicle behind and the calls of the others.

She opens his trousers and makes him erect, bounds on and off him, brings him into her gut, spears herself with him.

He is ashamed. Her fury does not break, even when he has burst inside of her. He thinks of her body stained with tears and dirt. He sees an image. Their abdomens are stuck together and for the first time he feels the indentation of her touch, then some sort of lasso around their melded trunks. He wants to jump up; he is so grateful. He wants to roll her thin body in dirt and hear the words fall from his mouth, *I cherish you.*

*

After prayers Cissé follows a trafficked road leading to a boulevard that crosses the city. The wound from the dog bite sends small arrows up his leg as he walks. He raises his shift and looks at the jagged skin. A woman passes, a tier of folded cloth on her head. She clucks her tongue as she rolls by. Cissé releases the shift onto the sand. He does not yet feel fever. Cissé's life began upcountry by the rivers. It is not true that he lived here as an adolescent. Delivered by an older brother to his uncle's compound in Bamako, it was thought that Cissé would gather fare money from passersby, for one of the uncle's many buses that roped through the town. But on Cissé's first night the uncle made use of the boy in a violent way, then whipped his buttocks with his belt. Cissé had been twelve years old when he ran away to the south.

Cissé cannot remember the face of his mother.

He reaches the main boulevard where minibuses fly past and cars stream at speed across all the lanes. People in the buses sit hunched forward and he sees a goat in a woman's arms. When he had run away south the minibus had lurched before a piglet squealing over the road, then fallen into a ditch where it lay upended. A large suffering woman had pinned Cissé beneath her. This woman pushed his bones together until he was an airless shape. At night, he wakes with the weight of this woman upon him.

A ticket boy hanging out of a minibus waves bills in his face and urges him to get on. Calls him a stupid shepherd when he just stands there.

He sits down. The bars and shops all along here are French. He drinks another Sprite and it is warmer than the one they gave him at the house. He eats a croissant which tastes of oily salt. He throws it down and asks the girl to get him a sweet cake.

At first, Cissé had thought that the white woman was interested in him as a man. He had worn a checked shirt under his shift, purchased from the Indian stalls. He had sprayed on perfume when he brought his wares to her house. The boy played outside but she disregarded his wild running.

When she had asked him to accompany them on the drive north he had said, *Of course, Bamako, je la connais.*

Cissé told them he has family to stay with in Bamako. But he has no one here. When a beggar comes up he asks him where he can buy something that will ease the pain in his foot. Something fast, something cheap. The fever has started in his spine. He follows this crumpled man into the back streets.

*

She awakes thinking they should never have come here

together. She looks at Sami's slow fan turning. Their skins do not touch. She knows he wants to photograph Maryam's rolling, splendid body. She has been there when it flared in him, the desire to approach subjects for his work. Once, two women in a slum bar drunkenly began to kiss. He bought them beers and asked the women if he could snap them. It was arousing, a courting. They were young with bright white teeth. She had watched his dance around them as tongues flickered, as cheeks and breasts were touched. She had asked him if he'd had a hard-on. He'd said his work never made him hard. He said it wasn't that at all.

She didn't believe this. Watching these two women with their bold dresses and market shoes had made her slippery wet.

He had produced an astounding sepia image of two dissolving profiles. The magnificence of closed eyelids; granular planes beneath the promontories of cheeks. The connection of a kiss. She could never have foreseen this vision.

She regrets flailing on the grass yesterday, begging him to photograph her. She is so desperate to enter the canon of his work. Flattened on the burning grass, the sunlight a vicious bath on her torso, she had thought she was granting him an image. But as she lay there she saw she had no understanding of what he sought, of how it became disinterred. He had clicked a few times, even bent to her, but his eyes had refuted her and grown annoyed. He had not even wanted her sex. Today, she will ruin those negatives.

She rubs her spit onto his curled fingers and pushes them inside of her, feels them enliven.

As they fuck she thinks of Maryam's nude body. She thinks of Kitty's photograph turned to the wall. She thinks of Maryam's purple vulva. She climaxes in a gradual, head-kicking way, feels herself spurt onto him; he licks her face and she feels choked.

She thinks that Cissé hasn't turned up, even though he said he would come after morning prayers.

The boy wakes when her lover goes off to shower and she wonders if, in the future, she can make amends. She still thinks there is a window where she can. The boy does not pull across the netting and come to her. He lies staring upward, little legs bent and hair she cannot bear to cut straying on the pillow.

The boy tells her that Cissé was bitten by a dog.

*

Sami provides them with a young man who will shepherd them through the city to where the musician lives. The interview is today. The photographer looks for Maryam along the hall where Sami's bedroom is located. But the bedroom door is closed. Sami wears an indigo blue shirt with ironing creases and embroidered filigree on the pockets. The photographer imagines this is a shirt that Maryam has given him recently. Sami does not speak of Maryam and their conversation resumes where it had left off before Maryam arrived at the house. Sami says he is working with a subject today, a woman who was kidnapped as a girl by the Tuaregs in the north, and held for nine years on the rim of the Sahara. He says he met this woman selling dried fish, there was a captive isolation in her eyes. The photographer is listening, he has often seen these sentiments within his subjects' eyes; his passion lies in the extrication of this.

The woman interrupts the two men talking and says that if Cissé doesn't turn up they will go without him, and good luck to him. She will manage with her French.

Her equipment bag is at the door with her dictaphone and battery charger.

The boy is grumpy and will not eat his food.

The woman's parts are swollen and burning and her lover extends his hand with long fingers and bitten-down fingernails across the table. He rests it on her forearm. The textures of their two skins meet.

Maryam appears in the hallway. Her hair is unmoved, the same weighted sculpture as it was last night, and she has little yellow balls of sleep in the corners of her eyes. Her body sways under her caftan and her breath is thick and stale. Maryam comes to the table and folds herself next to the small boy, asks him if she can share his breakfast. She and the boy eat up mango slices, then divide a roll of fleecy white bread with groundnut paste. Maryam asks the boy if she can touch his hair and he says *yes*.

At the gate, Cissé is leaning against a cinnamon tree in the shade.

*

The photographer drives out onto a thoroughfare. The woman and her son are beside him. Sami's guide sits in the back seat with Cissé. It feels strange to be driving again after being static in the house. Sami has said that they can return there to sleep, but he does not like to turn back, ever. He feels uncomfortable about the violence of their rapport this morning in Sami's converted garage. It feels like his come is still seeping out of him, as though there is a leak he cannot stop into his jeans, onto the seat. He touches his balls and his pants are dry. He wants to tell her, *We don't have to be like this.*

He remembers in the beginning, she asked him to

enter her when she was bleeding and this disgusted him though he had done it, then watched his red member subsiding on her stained belly. He wants to tell her, *This can stop.*

The photographer looks into the mirror and asks Cissé how was his family. Cissé replies that they were well and happy to see him. From a polythene shopping bag he draws a hand towel and passes it to the woman in the front seat.

'From my mother,' Cissé says to her.

The woman thanks him. But she turns around and says, 'Were you bitten by a dog? My son woke up saying you were bitten by a dog. Is that true?'

Cissé sinks back, laughs. He knows they would take him to some clinic and leave him there. Then the injections would start. The nurses, they would trouble him.

'No Madam, that is not true.'

She tells him she doesn't need his help for the interview.

The musk contours of the city air rise into the sky. There are monuments that look like bones scraped together, and many beaten-up cars. The minibuses scissor between them. There is a stream of heads along the footpath.

When they have been driving for an hour Sami's guide indicates a red wall where a road narrows, each side banked with orange sand. For the last thirty minutes they have passed along many streets like this. Sami's guide steps down from the jeep and walks away. The wall has an opening onto a courtyard where they see three women sitting on plastic chairs, a girl bent over sweeping, a stunted tree.

*

They follow the musician's youngest wife into the broad house, along dark halls and past rooms where voices murmur or children take spreadeagled naps on the floor. There is pounding somewhere, a long wooden pestle driven into a pulp, massaged around a mortar by swift hands. The journalist knows this much. She smells sauce boiling away, she thinks it is with dried fish or smoky crushed prawns. With the bitterness of leaves, baobab leaves perhaps. She checks the boy is following them. The photographer's equipment bag whistles against his thigh. The walls are bare and dusty, an impermanent substance. Her nipples contract with the slight chill, she feels it cross her shoulders. On the sleeve of the CD they gave her, the whites of the musician's eyes have been unrealistically enhanced.

The musician is hooked up to a drip in one of the back rooms. He lies on a mattress on the floor and does not respond when his wife calls him. She raises her voice. The man snuffles and hoists himself onto an elbow.

The dark room smells of illness, even shit. Apart from the mattress and drip stand, there is a chest of drawers piled with papers and rubbish; a mound of clothes on the cement floor and a bucket. The musician wears a turban and his black shift ripples into his skin. He looks at them. The photographer wants to pull out his camera.

The musician's wife tells them that her husband has typhus and they should not go too close. She says he is catching the plane to Denmark this evening and clucks her tongue. He has a big concert in two days. She says she has to cook now and the boy should come with her outside. The journalist tells the boy to go with her.

The couple take small steps further into the room and settle their bags on the floor. The journalist introduces herself. The photographer kneels to his bag, changes a lens. The silver rims slide together.

She cannot decide whether she should crouch or stand to take her notes. She sits cross-legged on the floor, opening her notepad, running over the points she has made and the brief the record company gave her, months back. She has been warned not to mention the old guy, the mentor. They are at loggerheads now. She prepares her dictaphone.

The photographer wants to capture the stench of sickness. He sees compressions of inky colour. The man's mouth opens and it is a deep rose cage.

The woman is offset by the way the limber photographer moves. She studies the musician, looking for the image that she will see printed, framed on a wall, far from here. She has worked with photographers before, but it usually comes after the interview, when the subject is fatigued and barriers fallen. She wants to tell the photographer to pull back, to give her some space, but he has seen something and she no longer exists, none of them do, it is just the light flare on a screen of chemicals, the unalterable narrative of exposure.

She says her lover's name. Asks him to leave the room and let her do her work.

The musician watches their discomfort.

She changes position, sitting back on her haunches. There are chinks of midday light scattered close to the wall beneath the half-closed shutters. The musician rolls a joint, lights up and inhales a couple of times, tugging on the tube so that the drip stand shivers. He holds out the smoking thing towards her. She rises on her knees and takes it.

She sits back, pulls up her spine, feels in command.

.

*

The photographer hears the boy's voice out in the courtyard between buildings. He is thinking of Maryam and her body smeared by the night of lovemaking. Maryam's stale smell runs along his nerves. Like his lover in the past, he wants to photograph her crouched, rinsing her body, an intimate ellipse.

Cissé sits in the shade on one of the plastic chairs, given to him by a woman with lavish gold earrings. He has a chewing stick in his mouth. The musician's young wife settles the boy by her as she squats on a stool over her pots. The boy asks where are her children, so that he might play. He asks her over and over again. Cissé guesses that she is childless or has recently lost a child. He knows the musician makes her work hard for him, harder than his older wives. He thinks the musician has given her an illness that the doctor said has damaged her womb.

The young wife slaps the face of the white child.

The photographer hears the boy crying out in the daylight. He throws his bag over his shoulder and hurries on. He sees the boy nursing his cheek and the young woman storms into the kitchen rooms.

The boy hugs him hard and a knot rises in the photographer's throat. He was abandoned in a boarding school in England when he was four. In the summer his mother, who was a diplomat, never arrived. He was farmed out to older couples who lived in silent houses and devised games.

'Come with me,' the photographer says to the stricken face.

In a corner of the blue-painted veranda the photographer deposits his bag and notices an overturned calabash and a four-legged cooking stool.

He places them before the intersecting blue planes; they are glazed by reverberated light. He sets up his Hasselblad, inching around the composition until the tension peaks between objects. He shows the boy the screen, makes him listen to the collapse of the shutter.

He asks the boy to go to the stool. The grooved calabash sits overturned by his dirty knees and his cascade of blond hair falls sweaty around his face. There are dark rings under the child's eyes he has never noticed. The boy sits with hands clasped.

He tells the boy more about the camera, given to him by a German photographer before he returned to Berlin. This man had one night invited him to a beach bar, and they had taken their beer bottles onto the sand. The German had pulled him to his body and kissed him as he fought. A strong, straight-backed man, he had released his shoulders and walked off into the dark.

The boy jumps up and pins a gecko to the wall.

He looks down at the box of the camera, rubs his thumb over one of the sides. He does not feel the photographs he took of the musician are worthy. He knows the images will be lifeless and flat. He thinks that to photograph his lover, he will have to wound her. Then revive her, resuscitate her. He feels love in his groin.

The boy shows him the gecko in his palm. He pulls up his shirt and entices the gecko onto his abdomen. It adheres there, pulsing. 'Snap me! Snap me!' he says. The boy calls over to Cissé to see. Cissé's chair is banked against a wall but he is watching. He throws up a hand that fans the air.

The journalist comes out of the doorway into the courtyard. Her breasts are free and her nipples pointed, her jeans edged in red dust. Cissé sees the other women look across at her as an unkempt idol from Europe, they know the musician will go there and fuck women like this.

She locates her son and her lover on the veranda. She pauses, observes the man kneeling, the boy holding up his shirt. All along she had tried to get the musician to talk, while the man released toneless answers. The musician has suggested they follow him to the airport and finish up at the VIP room inside. She isn't sure, but perhaps she heard the boy crying before.

'What are you doing to him?' she says to the photographer.

The boy sees her and begins to cry. She rushes to him and his embrace feels awful, an endless pledge. He will not tell her what is the matter.

'I think you can put that away now,' she says, indicating the camera between her lover's legs.

The young wife slips outside and tends to her pots. She gives the journalist an extraordinary smile and says they are welcome to eat. She says her baobab leaf stew is the best in the quartier. She invites them to sit down and commence washing their hands. Cissé wanders over.

As they eat in a wordless group the musician passes through the compound and the journalist sees the majestic man at his full height. He is dressed in smart jeans and a printed shirt, he wears sunglasses and carries nothing. The women on the plastic chairs watch him move. He speaks to no one. They hear a jeep revving outside the walls.

At the airport they have no access to the private lot where they can see the musician's jeep is stationed. The woman shows her press card which is looked over and handed back. None of the guards will tell them where the famous man has gone. The interview is suspended and they buy iced yoghurt sachets from a seller on the street.

*

The escarpment of Bandiagara rises above the Sahel plains, pocked with the pillbox granaries of the Dogon. Here, the god Amma gave life to the brown clay of the Earth and produced twins called Nommo, hermaphrodite fish-like beings. To establish gender, the twins were circumcised. The foreskin of the male became a black and white lizard; from the excised clitoris and labia minora of the woman, the first scorpion was born.

That night, they drive across this highland. They have visited Mopti, a Venice on the banks of the Niger. They stood before the adobe mosque with her brown vertical fingers. For the first time the journalist is stared at in a different way. Her boldness flutters and she wants to cover herself.

They have little money left and the photographer's half-brother in the U.K. sends them a transfer. She has almost finished her travel funds from the record company. They are going to drive all night, hopefully make it to the border.

The photographer is at the wheel. He feels relaxed, the woman is placid at this altitude, far away from Bamako. The landscape is a lunar surface. The road is singular, tossed over glades tessellated with glowing rocks. He would be content to stand out there in the wind, and speak of the arc of these days with her.

The woman's hand rests on her belly. She recognises changes in her breasts and skin and knows he has left his seed within her. He has told her there are twins in his family. Conceived here, in this land where twins embody the cardinal forces of the cosmos. She thinks: this has to stop when they get back. She is getting rid of these beads inside of her.

As they drive Cissé sees two men walking, they are wearing tall wooden masks that reach into the black sky. Their robes are flattened against their bodies. It is clear that they are spirits roving the earth. Cissé's ankle sends a charge through his body.

The photographer stops the car on a broad stretch, he wants to walk with her. The couple walk ahead a while along the lightless road. The wind enwraps them, it is stronger than he had thought; it whirs and vibrates. She turns around to look at the car tilted on the verge.

'Why? Why?' she says. 'We must go back.' She is not thinking of the sleeping boy, she is thinking that this place is too immense for them, too primordial. She wants the enclosure of the vehicle, the boy within her limbs. She would rather endure smaller things.

She remembers that the Dogon people discovered a hidden star, a blind star, using knowledge sifted down from the Egyptians, knowledge that the Westerners pored over and found a way to dismantle. There is a cloud of stars over them, galaxies printed upon galaxies, a celestial harvesting.

He holds her, feels her vehemence, asks her to be one with him.

She freezes up; looks skyward. Returns to his face and says *no*. All the same she expects him to pull down her jeans and bank into her. She anticipates the entry of his cock and feels alarmed when his hands desert her body. He leads her back to the car.

Later, at the border, the soldiers will not allow them to pass. They are told to park and wait until the dawn. The boy awakens, cries, is settled again. Cissé takes a woven blanket that she has bought and sleeps outside against a building. She touches her lover's face, he sucks her fingertip and turns away. She moves to the back seat with the child.

She cannot sleep. She sits awake watching Cissé twitching against the shed. It is hot and mosquitoes sail across the blue air in the car. The hours are motionless. They deliver a steep sense of direct being, so that she feels expanded into the atmosphere, the rubbish along the roadside, the lifeless flag and the barbed wire fence.

Before dawn, she detaches from the sleeping child and sits up behind him. She reaches over, embraces his skull, crams the features of his face, inhales his forehead, licks his temple.

Into his ear, she whispers.

Barbara Robinson

Supersum

I close the door behind me with a near-silent click, standing still for a moment in case the sound triggers mum's spring-trap reflexes and brings her back to life. But no, she must be asleep, or placating him. I walk away from that house on tired, shaking legs. I'm wearing those sunglasses – even though it's not light yet – the ones that you gave me that sunny day. The day we smoked a spliff on the field and lay on the blanket that you had brought. 'Wear these,' you said. 'Then they won't see your eyes when you get home.' We lay there, our elbows touching, giggling at nothing. Buzzed in the sunshine. *Amo, amas, amamus.* I love, you love, we love.

I walk down our street and I can hear the stop-start drone of the milk float. I know I have a long way to go and no money, so I try to get into a stride. My jeans are loose because I left my belt behind and I have to hitch them up every few seconds. He took mine to use against me when he couldn't find his own. I feel rage like lava rise from my belly to my throat when I remember. I keep walking. My fingers bunch my waistband to stop my jeans from falling down. 'You lanky streak of piss. You fucking little puff.' I keep walking.

There are broken settees in the alleyways and old tellies. There's always something that somebody doesn't need, left behind for somebody else to clear up. I'm getting nearer to the main road now. I'll walk along that main road to you, but I'll need to cross town first. Then it's a zig-zag line to your house. I think I can remember the way, even though I've only been once. When you gave me nice food from your fridge. Your dad smiled at me through his glasses and your mum hugged me when I left. 'Come again.' I think of your face and how it will look when I arrive at your house and that makes me touch my own. The skin rises to my fingertips like the bread your mum baked that day while we sat at the kitchen table. It feels like there's broken glass under my skin. I'm a human maraca. Don't shake me, though. *Doleo.* I hurt.

I turn onto the main road now and see some people waiting at bus stops or walking to work. Blinking and yawning, but fresh from rest and the shower. Early birds, unlike me. It's getting lighter now: pink threading the blue as the sky begins to sparkle. Now I have a reason for the sunglasses. One of those motorised sweepers is cleaning away the broken glass and food from last night. I think of the broken glass on our kitchen floor and mum trying to pick it up so nobody gets hurt but her eyes are swollen shut and her hands are shaking so much that she cuts herself. I feel myself start to cry but nothing comes. *Ambulo.* I walk.

I pass under the railway bridge and the air feels cool and damp. I cough and the sound echoes so I try a 'Hello!' My voice sounds thick and I wonder if my nose is broken. I can taste blood at the back of my throat. Suddenly I need to spit and when I do I see that there is blood in the gobbet of mucus, like a shining ruby amongst the pigeon shit on the ground. I lift my sunglasses to get a better look. The words 'DEANO IS A CUNT' are written in white on the wall of the bridge. 'You little cunt, you'll be fucking sorry you did that.' My jeans seem to be getting looser and I push my fists into the pockets to try and hold them up that way. It probably looks like I'm playing with myself and the thought of this brings a sob of laughter which makes me sound a bit mad.

The approach to town is a straight road with low terraced houses on both sides and very little shade and I'm grateful for how warm the sun feels on my skin. I think about lying next to you on the blanket that day. (I think about it all the time.) It felt natural to move closer to you and put my hand on the bare skin of your belly where your up-stretched arms had caused your tee-shirt to rise. You lifted your hips slightly and when they landed you were even closer to me. I allowed my fingers to move under your tee-shirt and so did you. You kissed the top of my head and – incredibly, given how close we were – we dozed. *Dormio, dormis, dormimus.* I sleep, you sleep, we sleep.

I walk past the train station and the large hotels and department stores. There is more debris on the streets here: the Saturday morning after the Friday night. It suddenly occurs to me that you and your family might not be awake; you might be having a lie-in after a relaxing evening of TV and wine. I've always hated Fridays since I was a little kid. That's when things would happen: on Friday or Saturday. Things would get broken: ornaments; cups; bones. Sometimes it's just name-calling. Just. 'You fucking puff. Should never have let you go to that fucking posh school. Fucking Latin.' But I love Latin. Latin is where I met you. You chose it because you're going to be a doctor like your dad and I chose it because I'm not going to be a twat like mine. *Supersum.* I survive.

I leave the built-up area of the centre and walk into the cleaner streets of your side of town. Past the antique shops and the delicatessens and the shops selling musical instruments. It's cloudy now. I'm feeling nervous. Sick with nerves and hunger. Worried about what you will say. Worried that you might send me away. I'm never going back there. She'll have to look after herself, now. I imagine her, trying to soothe him after his tantrum, hushing his apologies. I think of her broken body doing things that will only hurt her more.

The clouds are dark and I can feel drops of rain on my head and my bare arms. There's rain on my sunglasses and I have to wipe it away so that I can see. I'm coming down from the adrenalin of standing up to him. Standing and not cowering. Standing my ground. *Sto, stat.* I stand, he stands.

I turn right onto the road that lets me know I'm on the last part of my journey to you. The ancient trees umbrella me, giving some shelter from the spotty rain. I know where I am. The road doglegs sharply and leads into a neat little snicket that opens onto the area that you call The Avenues: one wide, straight road with avenues at right angles to it and a fountain at each intersection. There are three fountains to pass before I get to you. My legs are wobbly and I begin to shiver in the light rain. None of the clean, mild people walking their dogs and carrying their newspapers look at me. They probably think I'm a smackhead. I pass one fountain. I realise I'm not walking in a straight line but weaving across the pavement. I keep walking. Past the second fountain. I feel my nose running and I wipe it and when I pull my hand away there's blood on my fingers. I wipe them on my jeans. I reach the third fountain. I feel very small. *Timeo.* I am afraid.

I turn right onto the avenue that I know is yours. It seems so familiar but also different because I'm not with you. I pass the newsagent that sells peaches, tins of artichokes and squid in ink sauce. If I had some money I would buy you chocolate, or flowers for your mum. I know the house number: it's forty-four. I slow down now, thinking that this is a very bad idea. I want to change my mind. *Revoco.* I withdraw.

But then I see your house and something about the dark green door summons me. I open the wooden gate and make my way up the path. I raise my hand to lift the knocker and the door opens before I do. Your dad is standing there: one hand on the door and the other holding a hessian shopping bag. He says 'Um…' and then he goes back into the house but leaves the door open. I suddenly need the toilet. Your mum appears with her hair loose and she's wearing a soft-looking blue dressing gown. She puts her arm around my shoulders and pulls me in, closing the door behind me. She opens the door to a room off the hallway and leads me by the hand to the sofa. I'm still wearing the sunglasses and I can't see very much. She puts a cushion behind my head before she leaves. I must have dozed off because suddenly she is there again with a bowl of water. Gently, she removes the sunglasses. Our eyes meet and hers become moist. She uses a damp flannel to clean my face and although I know she's being gentle, it hurts so much that I begin to cry. *Lavat.* She washes.

Then the door opens and you're standing there wearing a long Snoopy tee-shirt, your eyes puffy with sleep. 'Fucking hell, what's he done to you?' You kneel on the floor as your mum shushes you and tells you there's no need for that language. She says I should sleep. She will make up the spare bed for me and some toast. She says I must stay here for a while. When she leaves the room you sit next to me on your parents' sofa and you hold my hand. I lift your hand to my mouth and kiss it. Then you kiss mine. *Osculor, oscularis, osculamur.* I kiss, you kiss, we kiss.

Tracy Fells

Twisted

Granddad was having a bit of a turn. Mum didn't want a gaggle of giggling little girls upsetting him. Her party was cancelled and Alice had to be grown up about it. The doctor had called earlier and now Granddad needed peace and quiet. Alice picked the eight candles off the birthday cake one by one, licking the pink fondant icing from the spikes of the plastic holders. Under Mum's direction she cut a wedge out of the plain Victoria sponge, lipstick-red jam sticking to her fingers.

'A nice big slice,' said Mum, her long flat brown hair falling forward over her shoulders. 'This is for Granddad, remember. He loves my sponge cake.'

'Pigs will eat anything,' said Auntie Ruth. Her hand rested gently on the back of Alice's head. 'Don't you think the birthday girl should get first dibs on her own cake?' She mouthed something to Mum, something like *stop putting the stinking old goat first.* Alice loved Auntie Ruth, because she said exactly what she was thinking, even if it was a bit rude.

Auntie Ruth had made a special trip, because it was Alice's birthday, and was staying for the whole week. This made up for the party being cancelled. It made up for a lot.

'You can take it in to Granddad.' Mum toppled the slice onto a pink paper plate, holding it out to Alice. 'Ruthie will bring along his cup of tea in a minute.'

Granddad lived on the ground floor in what used to be the dining room. A big square room with double doors that could open out onto the patio, but never did. Heavy mud-brown drapes kept the sun away. Alice thought his room always smelled of wee. With his metal three-legged frame, Granddad could just about get around unsupervised. He could hobble to the downstairs loo, but he often left the door open. Once she'd caught sight of his pyjama bottoms pooling around his slippers as he stood before the toilet. She'd squeezed her eyes tight. A motorised chair carried him upstairs to the main bathroom, where Mum had fitted a special bath seat that went up and down like the stair lift. Alice liked playing with the bath seat, whizzing Benjy the cat up and down, until Mum caught her and slapped the back of her legs.

He was usually napping when she was sent to his room on some errand. Propped up on pillows, mouth drooping and the remains of his last meal dribbling down his chin. She could creep in and out without having to go near the bed. That afternoon he was awake. He blinked at her.

'How about a birthday kiss?' Granddad tapped a shaky finger on his purple-streaked cheek.

She had to lean on the knobbly, custard-coloured bedspread to kiss him. Alice felt the scratch of bristles on her lips. A wrinkled hand snaked up under the frilly hem of the new party dress Mum was letting her wear all day, since it was her birthday.

A strangled screech came from behind her. Auntie Ruth had followed with the promised cup of tea. The cup and saucer fell to the carpet, splashing lukewarm tea across the pink satin of Alice's dress. The cake slid from its plate, falling into jammy clumps on her ballet pumps.

*

'What about your dad, Alice? I asked for an early memory of when your family was all together, but you haven't mentioned him.' The counsellor's sleek black plait fell forward over her pale blue blouse. The colour suited her. Leena always dressed smartly, skirt or trousers and a simple, plain blouse. Alice wondered if she changed into a sari when she got home, when she was "off-duty". 'Was your dad still living with you and your mum?'

'Good question.' She paused for as long as possible, but Leena had more patience, never jumping into the silence. 'I hardly remember him. He never says or does anything, like one of those extras hanging around the market in Eastenders.' Alice crossed her legs to match Leena's posture. Mirroring was an easy technique to mimic, one she'd pinched from an online guide to active listening. She hoped to annoy her, but so far Leena appeared unmoved by the mockery.

Cupping light brown hands on her navy-blue skirt Leena continued, 'Isn't it possible he was at work? He was running your grandfather's business. That must have kept him away from home a lot of the time.' Leena perfectly recalled all their previous meetings, yet never took notes, causing Alice to question whether their conversations were being taped. She could only do that with the client's permission - Alice was pretty certain about that.

'S'pose. I do remember something – he used to shoot squirrels in the woods. Once he brought back a squirrel's tail. The stump was bloody and gristly, where he'd cut it off.' She shuddered. 'It was rank.'

Leena's gaze flicked away, above Alice's head. The tick-less clock was mounted on the wall behind Alice.

'My head feels like when your headphone leads get all knotted together in a drawer.' Alice propped her feet on the edge of the low table that sat between them. 'I tug them apart. This happened and then that happened … Aunt Ruth came home for the party that never happened … she fought with Mum. Granddad died. Then the police arrived-' Her foot almost nudged Leena's mug, hand painted with *Mummy* in childish clumsy letters '-When I go back to the drawer, the leads are tangled again.'

Leena moved the mug away from Alice's foot. 'Sometimes we recall exactly what we want or need to, but usually only when we are ready to remember. It's like pulling at a loose thread and then an entirely different string of memories comes tumbling out. The subconscious does a good job of protecting us by burying or hiding painful memories.'

'Brilliant,' said Alice, 'so my subconscious could be hiding something even more disturbing.'

'That's what we're here to find out.'

Alice, tired of the game, leaned back in her chair. 'I don't want to talk about my dad, not today.'

Leena nodded. 'Tell me about your community service.'

'Like what?' Alice looked away from Leena. There were no pictures on the walls, no family photographs on display, no knickknacks on the bookshelves. The walls were a pale mint green matching the carpet. The only personal item in Leena's office was the coffee mug. She didn't have to talk. They could sit in silence for the hour, but Alice had been warned this would mean an extension, more sessions would be scheduled and then more again, if necessary. 'We've spent the last three weeks digging bloody ditches. It's been mind-numbing.'

'How are you getting on with the rest of the group?'

Alice laughed. 'You'd love them; they're a therapist's dream. I don't want to talk about them.'

'We don't have to talk about them,' said Leena. 'Would you like to talk about your granddad's death?'

'That's a closed question!' Alice said with triumph. Leena rarely slipped up on the basics. 'I'll let you off for once. Go on, ask me another.' She pulled her feet off the table, making the coffee mug tremble.

Alice knew the interrogator's check-list of open

questions always began with: how, who, what, when ...

How did Granddad come to drown in the bath?

Who was responsible?

How did that make you feel? (One of Leena's favourites.)

What did you do to make your mother hate you?

When did you come to terms with your aunt being arrested for murder?

'You are here because you emptied your grandfather's ashes onto a bedspread and then tried to burn them.' continued Leena.

Auntie Ruth would have fired back the perfect retort, with appropriate sarcasm. 'Along with all the other indiscretions embarrassing my mother,' said Alice. 'Don't forget I nick cigarettes and skive school.'

'The resulting fire in your mum's bedroom could have burned the house down, Alice. What did you hope to achieve?'

Alice snatched up the painted mug and hurled it over Leena's head. It hit behind the desk, broke instantly, splattering cold coffee across the empty green wall.

Later, at the graffiti-plastered bus stop she thought how the dripping coffee had looked like one of those inkblot pictures you had to describe. Concentrating her thoughts on the stain Alice tried to forget the counsellor's wide, hurt eyes as Leena had remained motionless in her seat.

*

Alice sat with her shoulders pressed against the bedroom door. Benjy's tail twitched a silent beat as he slept in her lap. The voices of Mum and Auntie Ruth carried down the hallway, mainly because they were shouting. It was Granddad's bath night; Alice stayed well clear of this weekly event.

'Daddy would like you to bathe him tonight.' Mum's voice was shrill and spiky. Alice could picture her standing rigid with soapy hands on hips. 'It wouldn't hurt for you to help out with him around here. Just once, before you bugger off and leave me alone again.'

Auntie Ruth's reply echoed round the house. 'I'm not bathing that old git.' More words flew at Mum, most of them sounded rude, but few made any sense. Sometimes adults talked another language. 'You shouldn't leave an old man lying in a bath without supervision, Rachel, God forbid he slips under and can't get up. You'd better get back in there, before he has an accident.'

*

'Were those your aunt's exact words? Did she describe your grandfather as an "old git", or is this what you now imagine she would call him?' Leena swivelled round to take a sip from the cup of water, a plastic cup Alice noted, placed on the desk behind her. She wore a white blouse, an emerald silk scarf and tailored black trousers that accentuated her tiny waist.

'Is either relevant?' Alice stared at the wall, where the faint outline of last month's outburst lingered. 'What difference does it make to how I feel now?' Her latest distraction was to see how long she could keep the rally going. But Leena was an expert and the game grew dull.

'What happened when the police came for your aunt, can you tell me what you remember?'

Alice relaxed into the tub chair, crossing her long legs. 'Benjy was on the windowsill in my bedroom. I watched them walk her out to the car. Auntie Ruth's hands were handcuffed and the policewoman tugged her forwards. She put a hand on Auntie Ruth's head and pushed her down roughly inside. The next time I saw Auntie Ruth was three months ago, nine years later, when she came to stay with Mum and me.'

'After she'd been released?'

'Obviously. It took her two years to pluck up courage and come visit us. I'm glad she did.'

Alice had been honest with Leena about her memories. They were tangled like electrical leads, but each time she tugged, the more the leads twisted and tightened. Was she remembering Auntie Ruth's arrest frame by frame, as it happened, or replaying a childhood diet of TV police dramas?

*

A strand of blonde hair came loose as Ruth leant across to kiss her cheek. Alice thought her aunt's new look, a neat blonde bob, was pretty trendy and longed to touch the velvet band of shaven darker hair at the base of her neck. Aunt Ruth's skin smelled of freshly picked strawberries, but her breath held the sweet and sour of rotting apples.

'How would you like to come on holiday with me? Just the two of us for a couple of weeks,' whispered Ruth. Alice nodded fiercely. 'Your mum can cope with Granddad and we can have fun.' Auntie Ruth's eyes were bright, her smile filling the room. 'Tomorrow morning I'll sort out the details and we can start packing.'

She tucked the duvet under Alice's arms and kissed her again, this time on her centre parting. Alice thought this was the final goodnight kiss, but her aunt sank gently onto the bed beside her, squashing the tip of Benjy's tail. He mewed in complaint and moved further down to curl on Alice's feet. Looking round the room, decorated in a monochrome pink palette, Auntie Ruth added, 'Not all little girls have to be princesses. You can choose whatever you want to be. If you want to wear scarlet or paint your room black, that's okay with me.' She started to get up, but sat straight down again and squeezed Alice's hand. 'The angels and I will look out for you, Alice. And remember, not all angels have wings you can see.'

The next morning Alice heard strange voices downstairs, so she stopped at the bend in the staircase, beside the arched window. Curled like a comma on the glossy sill was her favourite place to sit and watch the weather roll over the South Downs. Alice clambered up in time to see Auntie Ruth and a black policewoman walk out to the police car. The policewoman's hand rested on the back of Auntie Ruth's denim jacket, as if guiding her forward. Auntie Ruth gripped her handbag in small white hands.

*

Leena made an audible sigh. 'So, there were no handcuffs. Your aunt walked unrestrained to the police car.'

'In each version the picture changes. I can't help that.' Alice snapped back, then mumbled, 'Thought these sessions were supposed to drag out the truth.'

'These sessions are to help you with your anger, to understand why you need to lash out.'

'I know why,' Alice said sharply. She breathed out and then smirked. 'What I really want is to stop chucking coffee mugs at people.'

Leena examined her nails; they were glossed, but unpainted, edged by crisp crescent moons. 'Why do you think you need to lash out?'

Alice stood. What was the point of carrying on with this farce when clearly Leena never listened? Her mother was a bully and Auntie Ruth had been a fucking lunatic fixated with angels, before she upgraded to a drunk.

'We still have another five minutes,' said Leena in a quiet, contained voice. She didn't blink, but her cheek muscles tightened.

Alice jabbed at the fading bruise on her own cheek. 'Why don't you ask why Mum did this?' With her hand on the door handle she turned back briefly. 'Why don't you ask me what happened after Auntie Ruth kissed me goodnight and before the police arrived in the morning?'

If Leena asked that question then maybe she would finally remember for herself. Auntie Ruth refused to fill in the gaps, refused to talk about that time.

Leena didn't move from her seat, which was a shame, as Alice wanted to see the woman's shoulder blades. To check for sprouting wing buds beneath the white cotton blouse.

*

The Lawsons' midsummer barbecue was legendary in Alice's cul-de-sac. Each year she secretly pretended that the party food and decorations were all for her - in honour of the birthday her mum no longer celebrated. The cake table wobbled under the weight of the chocolate fountain, lemon meringue tartlets and mini éclairs. Chinese lanterns and outdoor lights were woven around the large garden like Santa's summer grotto. Adults swatted away the circling wasps above Mr Lawson's homemade, and definitely not-for-kids, punch.

When she was younger Alice had commandeered the trampoline, ring-fenced with netting, as her happy place. She kicked off her sandals and bounced until she almost threw up, not caring who saw her knickers as her summer dress leapt with her into the blue sky. This year the barbecue was timed to coincide with the celebrations for the Lawsons' twenty-fifth wedding anniversary. Using her weekly allowance Alice had bought a new dress, which showed off her waxed, tanned legs. A manic, bald-headed clown replaced the bouncy castle as the children's entertainment, although his inappropriate squirting from a fake flower down the cleavage of several mothers wouldn't secure him a return gig. Alice, now in her teens, was too big for the trampoline, which sat forlorn and forgotten at the bottom of the garden, damp rose petals pooling in its saggy centre.

'Not bouncing today, Alice?' said Mr Lawson, standing way too close. He breathed beer and fried onions across the back of her neck. 'I loved watching you on the trampoline. You always look so happy, trying to touch the sky.'

'Don't you think I'm a bit old to be playing on trampolines, Mr Lawson?'

Handing Alice a plastic wine glass, almost over-flowing with punch, he winked overtly and added, 'A pretty girl is never too old to flash her knickers. And you are old enough now, Alice, to call me Peter.'

She shifted her weight, slouching away from him, and a thin strap slid off her bare shoulder. Alice suddenly wished she had worn a bra under the skin-tight scarlet dress. His fingers were warm, and smooth against her skin as they gently rolled the loose strap back into place. Since Auntie Ruth had gone away nobody touched her. Alice's only human contact was the occasional shove as somebody pushed her out of the way in the school corridors. Hours later, lying on top of her duvet, with Benjy curled into her side; she could still feel the weight and warmth of Mr Lawson's touch on her shoulder, glowing like a fluorescent handprint in the dark.

*

'I'm confused by the timeline, Alice. Is this a recent barbecue?' Leena's voice had a cool edge. She wove fingers together and cupped her hands.

'It was last year.'

'How old were you?'

Alice shrugged. 'Fifteen or sixteen, I guess.'

Leena was wearing heavy black-rimmed glasses, making her brown eyes seem rounder than usual. She hadn't worn them at any of their previous appointments and Alice wondered if Leena normally used disposable lenses. She was finding it hard to keep eye contact, her attention continually distracted to the shiny, ebony arms of the glasses hooked behind Leena's perfectly shaped ears.

'Were you under age?'

'No, the party must have been mid-July or later as it was celebrating their wedding anniversary. My sixteenth birthday had already happened.' She wriggled on the sticky chair causing the leopard print mini-skirt to ride up her bare legs making an uncomfortable squeak.

'Your next-door neighbour, Peter Lawson, seduced you during a party for his twenty-fifth wedding anniversary?'

'Don't you believe me?'

'I want to be clear on the facts, Alice.'

'We did it on my mum's bed. I had to shoo Benjy off first. Then he, Peter that is, put a towel over the duvet.'

'A towel?'

'In case I bled.' Alice put her feet up onto the low coffee table that kept them apart. 'He was being practical, you see.'

Natural daylight was leaking from the room, the sky darkening from white to grey then finally to black. At first the patter of rain on glass was gentle and haphazard like an afterthought, but grew quickly to a frenzied battering of tiny determined hailstones.

'It was your first time?'

'Shocking, huh?' Alice studied her own nails, uneven, plain and grubby. 'That I was still a virgin by my sixteenth birthday.'

'Did he get you drunk? You said he gave you punch.'

'No. I didn't touch a drop, was sober for the whole experience, which didn't last long.'

*

Peter Lawson's mouth stretched into a misshapen grimace, his eyes scrunched shut as he arched away from her. His breathing juddered, spluttering like a failing engine, making Alice think he was about to have a heart attack. But then he cried out loudly and slumped forwards gasping, a landed fish upon her chest. She dug her nails into his naked back, probing into muscle and fat. Alice couldn't feel anything beneath the flabby skin.

*

'Tell me more about this fascination for angels,' Leena asked, her voice uncharacteristically soft. 'Does this come from Auntie Ruth?'

Alice tucked her knees onto the chair, clasping her hands around them. 'I haven't found one yet.' She bowed her head, resting her chin on her knees, as if in prayer. 'I lied.'

Leena leant forwards. 'Lied about what?'

*

The leads untangled, spiraling apart. The drawer in her head was suddenly neat and tidy, each memory distinct and catalogued just waiting for inspection. The bathroom door swung backwards as Alice leant against it. Granddad was slumped on the bath seat; a whistling sound came from his open mouth. He'd fallen asleep in the soapy water.

*

'Benjy,' said Alice, lifting her head again. 'I lied about Benjy. We never had a cat. Mum hated animals.'

Leena gently touched the corner of one eye as if brushing away an eyelash. 'I understand why you needed to create him. We all need someone or something to cherish.'

Alice tried to scratch at the itch pushing through her shoulder blades. She gave up and slid from the chair onto the green carpet.

*

Her mum was now shouting at Auntie Ruth on the landing. 'Why make such a fuss, Ruth? Daddy loves Alice.'

'Like he loved me?' Auntie Ruth's voice was almost a shriek.

'You always got special treatment, all the attention. And then you made up all those hateful stories.'

There was a loud crack and a thud as someone fell against the wall. Had Auntie Ruth hit Mum? Alice bumped into the bath, her bobbly dressing gown hooking on the seat mechanism. The safety catch was off.

There was another slapping sound. 'You and Mummy never believed me. I'm taking Alice away before he starts it all over again.'

Alice didn't understand what they were arguing about. She tugged her dressing gown free from the control panel; the bath seat began to whirr. Granddad's purple face sank under the water, his yellow-tipped fingers slipping and sliding against the plastic sides of the pink bath. He seemed unable to pull himself back up again.

She was too scared to call for help. If Mum found her there then she wouldn't be allowed to go on holiday with Auntie Ruth.

The water sloshed over the sides of the bath making little puddles on the tiles. Granddad was still under the surface, his eyes now open, staring up at the ceiling. He'd stopped thrashing about. A hand stroked the top of her head. Auntie Ruth was at her side.

'Go back to bed, Alice,' said Auntie Ruth softly. 'I'll look after Granddad.'

David Lewis

*The Mayes County Christmas Gun
Festival*

Two locations stand out at the festival: first is the field labeled *Grounds for Shooting*, second is Santa's Village. We're in line for the latter. Brennen, my husband, is browsing his smartphone, looking up positions in Modern Language departments. He received another rejection this morning. Happy Holidays. To complicate matters, I just got tenure. So while he looks for jobs, I'm minding his eight-year-old niece, Clarissa. Clarissa plans to ask Santa for a crossbow.

"Uncle Martin, do you and Uncle Brennen think Chicago is better than Oklahoma?"

"I thought we were talking about archery." It's challenging to keep her on one subject. "Where does one buy arrows for a crossbow?"

"Mine will shoot bolts. But my question was first," Clarissa has a habit of yelling when she speaks. "Is Oklahoma better?"

"We don't have festivals like this in Chicago."

Clarissa and her mother, Brennen's sister Gayle, both delight in uncomfortable conversations. Yesterday Brennen and I flew into Tulsa. After Gayle greeted us, Clarissa announced that she was going to see Santa at the *Christmas Guns*. "That's an idea," I said, thinking I could share her enthusiasm. Then Gayle suggested Brennen and I take Clarissa; it would be nice for her to spend time with her two uncles. "That's an idea," I said, thinking I could restrain her enthusiasm. But, to my surprise, Brennen agreed. He said he'd like to see how welcome two queers would be at his hometown's gun festival. "That's an idea," a horrifying one, I thought. After a tedious, passive-aggressive conversation between Brennen and his sister, Gayle promised that the festival wasn't a survivalist convention for homophobes: we'd be fine. Brennen snorted, which is his preferred gesture for deprecation, his kineme for disdain. "We'll see."

Fortunately, his sister's been proven right so far. Everyone's been hospitable. The experience has amended more than one of my outmoded *idées reçues* about gun enthusiasts. For instance, we met a charming shotgun owner who runs the festival's catfish stand. She spotted me and Brennen as a couple and asked if we were married. She was grinningly generous with our tartare sauce.

"Listen to this," Brennen frowns at his phone. I fear he isn't looking at job applications any more. "The Cloud Shoot is a German tradition, originally thought to frighten away evil spirits before Christmas." He ends with a snort. "German *mein Arsch!*" he shouts. I hope nobody's listening.

He swivels his head left to right like an owl looking for an argumentative mouse, a mouse who'd remind him that he was initially looking for university work. No mice here. I suspect he's planning another of his *lived-culture* essays. They always start with promise, but he lacks tenacity. His pieces are neither rigorous enough for academic publication, nor popular enough for general news outlets. They often end up in charming, digital holes-in-the-wall on the verge of bankruptcy.

"Uncle Martin," Clarissa says, "Will the guns scare away Santa?"

"I'm certain Santa is equipped for the occasion."

"Will they scare you?"

"No, why? Do I look frightened?"

"Mom said guns scare you."

"I don't want a gun. There's a difference."

Her mouth curls into a smile. "What if someone points a gun at you?"

"I'll do whatever they ask."

"Even a bad thing?"

"It depends on how bad," I say.

An elf in a green costume, shimmering like a polished tree bauble, advances up the line with a red bucket in hand. Bells on his shoes jingle as he walks.

"He's Santa's slave," Clarissa says.

"Young lady," Brennen looks up from his phone, "Don't you think that word is offensive?"

Clarissa looks confused.

"She didn't mean any harm," I say.

Brennen turns to me, ruffled and irritated. Before he can launch into a lecture, the elf approaches us and tips his candy-striped hat.

"Good afternoon Sirs. I'm collecting donations for the Kris Kringle Hometown Security fund."

He smells of peppermint and tobacco. His sky-blue eyes gleam above a week's stubble. He would be attractive if he lost weight. Before I can stutter an excuse, he positions his bucket near my chest.

"Come on buddy. Santa and the elves need practice ammo. To get the girl on Santa's lap, you've got to pay for shells and caps," he says, holding a thick index finger in the air.

A "Ha" erupts from Brennen. The whole line hears it. The elf's eyes narrow. It's up to me to defuse this. I give him my most professorial gaze and respond; as they say, an iamb for an iamb.

"Arm the elves with bullets and guns; boys and girls are in for some fun."

Blank stares all around, like my undergraduates.

Before I can pull out my wallet, Brennen speaks. "Sorry, but we've already paid for our tickets."

Clarissa looks at Brennen, then the elf, then me. "We're going to see Santa, aren't we?"

The elf leans in and whispers. "Listen fellas, this is

the county's only Santa. So let's keep off the naughty list and show the spirit of giving."

Brennen taps his smartphone. I hope he isn't recording this. The elf notices.

"Nice phone. You two brothers?"

Clarissa answers for us, like her mother would. "No, they aren't brothers. They're married. They're my uncles Martin and Brennen."

"Married uncles," the elf says. "Reckon that means you boys don't have guns."

Brennen fumes. "Could you repeat that? My husband's from Chicago and is used to complete sentences." His hands knot into fists.

I would give anything to disappear, or make Brennen disappear. Since I can't, I take out my wallet. Attention shifts to me.

"Martin, what are you doing?" Brennen's voice breaks.

Should I give a twenty? No, a ten is enough. The elf cracks his knuckles; extraordinary how he does it with one hand. No, not extraordinary, terrifying. I toss two twenties into the bucket. What does one say after donating to a militia?

"Sorry for the confusion. This ought to cock the rifles for you and Santa."

The elf examines the bills. His blue eyes sparkle and he tips his candy-striped hat at me. "Thanks Uncle." He winks and moves past Brennen as though he were invisible.

Brennen isn't happy. "What was that?" Though he's looking at me, his thumb still jabs and swipes the screen of his smartphone.

"Preemption," I say. "What would you suggest we do? Couldn't you hear his knuckles?"

"I've taken boxing classes, Martin."

"It's questionable whether auditing a *Hemingway-style* boxing course is going to serve you well outside of academia."

"Dr. Cole is an excellent self-defense teacher."

"Only if you're defending yourself against sobriety."

Clarissa tugs my hand. "Was that really one of Santa's elves?"

Brennen's locked in on my eyes. "Why don't you support me for once?"

"For once? Who bought our plane tickets here from Chicago? I've always supported you."

"Uncle Martin," Clarissa swings from my arm, "that wasn't–"

"Not for what counts," Brennen interrupts, "You didn't just now, not with that Yuletide Mafioso, not with my applications."

"So I'm to write your applications now? Be realistic, Brennen."

"Oh, now I'm not realistic."

"Uncle Martin," Clarissa whines.

"One moment Clarissa."

"Martin, you've become comfortable," Brennen snorts, "You've forgotten your principles, privately and professionally."

"No Brennen, I'm simply not delusional about my capabilities, privately and professionally." A pearl of sweat trickles down my forehead. The wind chills it.

"Uncle Martin." Clarissa's patting my hand. Her eyes are wide and desperate.

Brennen's silent, holding-his-breath silent.

"Yes, Clarissa?" I say, shivering.

"That man wasn't one of Santa's elves," she says.

The line inches forward.

*

While Clarissa is on Santa's lap, Brennen leaves, supposedly to look over a job opening, but more likely to sulk behind the Southern Fried Everything stand. Clarissa grimaces for her photo with Father Christmas, who then sends her away with a gravelly *Ho ho ho*. She stuffs her picture into a pocket and marches back to me.

"Was Santa nice? Did you get a good picture?" I say.

"He looks different from last year." She bites a finger and worries off a nail between her teeth. "Can elves make crossbows?"

"That's an interesting question. Let's think about it. First, what do we know about elves?"

I stall and stall until, finally, a distraction. Trumpets blare from the other end of the fairgrounds. Tinseled megaphones perched on the vendors' stands screech to life.

"All gun-carrying participants to the shooting grounds for the Fifth Annual Christmas Cloud Shoot."

The trumpets play a military-sounding *Rudolph the Red Nosed Reindeer*. The fairgoers perk up, as though they might launch into song; and from fanny packs, jackets, purses and socks, portfolios, beer bellies, bras and pockets, everyone pulls out their gun. The whole festival is armed.

I call Brennen but his phone directs me to his voicemail. *Hi, I can't answer or don't want to. Leave me a message and I'll get back to you if it's important.* I imagine potential employers throwing his application away after hearing that. Should I leave a message? I hang up. He'll find us. Clarissa and I follow the crowd until we see an empty patch of lawn for spectators. There are hundreds on the shooting field. Clarissa grabs my arm.

"Uncle Martin? Why don't we have our guns?"

I wonder if someone would lend me one.

"I don't carry a gun."

"Even nudists carry guns."

"That's interesting. What would they do with the gun if they needed both hands?"

"They'd put it in their butt." When Clarissa laughs, her cheeks jut out in sharp angles.

"That sounds too risky for me."

Fairgoers and stand vendors line up behind five ancient-looking cannons. I scan the crowd but can't find Brennen. Clarissa huffs.

"Next year, you aren't coming. Mom always has her gun."

I wonder if Gayle brought weapons into our home on her last visit to Chicago.

"We'll lodge that complaint with your mother."

The crowd stands apart, forming an aisle with the cannons at one end and Santa at the other. He's dressed differently. Apart from his red cap, he's exchanged his outfit for a grey Civil War uniform. He marches to the cannons, one hand carrying a bag of toys, the other a Confederate battle flag. Behind him the clear-eyed elf stands at attention with a rifle at his side. He's still wearing his green costume, shimmering like a polished beetle. The trumpets play the opening to *Dixie*. The crowd sings.

Oh, I wish I was in the land of cotton.
Old times there are not forgotten.
Look away, look away, look away Dixie Land.

Santa stands at attention by the row of cannons. I can't believe I'm witnessing this. I can't believe Brennen is missing this. I grab Clarissa's hand and squeeze.

"Ouch, Uncle Martin." She pulls her hand free.

The trumpets pick up the pace. The cannons, like coughing giants, punctuate the chorus with raspy explosions.

I wish I was in Dixie. Hooray! BOOM *Hooray!* BOOM

Clarissa screams and grabs my leg. Cannon smoke blankets the field; it smells of smoldering metal and burnt wire. A turbulent energy thunders through the air. Santa pulls an antique rifle out of his bag of toys and fires at the sky. His elf howls and shoots immediately after him, setting off the crowd. Hundreds of fairgoers fire at the clouds. The air is popping with gunshots. My arm hair stands, rigid and electric. Clarissa is hugging my leg, screaming and laughing. I wish I'd brought a gun. I'd buy one now. I'd launch a bullet soaring into the sky and feel the detonation in my hands.

A hand falls on my shoulder. It's Brennen.

"Brennen, have you been watching this?"

He's trying to meet my eyes and look around me at the same time. When he responds, I can't hear him over the gunshots. It sounds like *hard to believe.*

"Isn't it just?" I say as though I'd understood.

He grabs my shoulder and pulls me closer. His fingers grip like talons. This time he yells. "We have to leave!"

Clarissa is jumping around us, whooping out hysterical laughs, tears running down her smiling face.

"I thought you wanted to see this!" I shout to Brennen over the gunfire.

"I took back our bribe money from that crook," he says.

"What crook?"

He nods at the shooting field. In the swarm of brown and black coats, I see the elf's green costume, shimmering like a polished bullet.

"You took the militia money?" I imagine the crowd turning to us, setting their sights–

Cannon fire. BOOM

Brennen rolls his eyes. "Let's go to the car."

"You stole money from a militia," I say.

"You're repeating yourself, Martin. Don't be so surprised. It's fine. We'll donate it."

"But you stole it."

"You can't rob a robber."

"I don't think that argument will hold up in court."

The gun shots are thinning out. They sound more dangerous without the cacophony of constant firing. I imagine the shooters taking careful aim at us. Brennen grabs my arm.

"We have to leave."

I take Clarissa's hand, but she pulls away.

"We can't go now, Uncle Martin."

Brennen runs ahead to the parking lot, abandoning me with his niece again. I kneel down, look her in her round, trusting face and lie.

"Clarissa, if you come along, I'll bet Santa will get you that crossbow."

Her mouth purses into a furious wrinkle. "Liar!"

"Clarissa, sweetheart, we have to go." I can't suppress the saccharine tone my voice adopts. She crosses her arms and plants herself in place like a stubborn garden gnome. I'll have to pick her up and carry her to the car lot.

When I seize her waist, her eyes widen and for a moment she's too shocked to resist. Then she kicks and screams. Her shriek curdles her face into a starburst of furrows and lines. I hadn't expected this. It's mortifying. I must look like a kidnapper. I set her back down but she isn't appeased. She repays my surrender by socking me in the crotch. Sharp, ragged pain doubles me over. As she runs after Brennen, I lie on the ground and bite my tongue, holding on to – I hope – a minimum of dignity.

I stand up as the pain ebbs into a tender ache and glance back at the field. Nobody is looking in my direction. The crowd's dispersing. The elf is gone. A few stragglers continue firing at the sky, their isolated gunshots raising thoughts of vigilante executions. Walking to the parking lot, each step is a needling flare in my groin. Another gunshot. I walk faster. The sky is dark-grey, as if the bullets were blackening the clouds. I walk faster.

I reach Brennen and Clarissa outside the entrance to the parking lot. Then I see the elf, leaning against a post, smoking, his costume shimmering like polished menace. He's cradling his rifle under one arm. When I arrive, he tips his candy-striped hat and stamps out his cigarette.

"Hello there Uncles."

We stare like reindeer in the headlights, reindeer who have stolen the Kris Kringle Hometown Security Fund. His shoe bells jingle as he pushes off from the post.

"How'd you folks like the cloud shoot?"

Clarissa responds. "It was spectacular."

The elf leisurely jingles up to her. "It sure was." He crouches to her eye level, holding his rifle to the side. "Would you believe that in these last five years, we've only had one incident."

He puts a hand on her shoulder and stares at Brennen. "One year, a couple fellas thought they'd steal the donations bucket." He looks back at Clarissa. "What would you do with those two bandits, little lady?"

She turns to us then the elf. "Put them in jail?"

The elf chuckles. "I suppose so. You'd have to knock their wind out first."

My mind's blank, white as panic. I fight the urge to

drop to the ground.

"Can elves make crossbows?" Clarissa asks.

"Elves are magic," he says.

Magically, Clarissa accepts that. She bows her head to her chest, looks at me, then the elf, and frowns. "Did you shoot the bandits?" There's a tremor in her voice, the kind announcing tears.

"No, little lady, no. Now don't cry. Nobody's getting shot. Hey speaking of shooting, how would you like to fire this?" He holds out his rifle. "Do you think the uncles would let you?"

Her eyes widen and she shakes her head no. The elf looks at us.

"No? That wouldn't be nice, would it? That's taking all the fun out of a Cloud Shoot." His face hardens. "That's almost like stealing."

Brennen takes a breath. He's about to say something. I cut him off.

"You know what, Mr..."

"Sparkles."

"Mr. Sparkles, Clarissa would love that. You'd make her day. Now, Clarissa, will you promise not to tell your mother about Mr. Sparkles and the gun?"

Her face becomes serious. She shakes her head no, which I presume means yes. But that's irrelevant. Brennen shakes his head no, which I presume means NO. He's looking right at me as if Clarissa and the elf weren't there, as if this had nothing to do with them, as if this wasn't about guns, or Christmas, or right or wrong; as if this was about us alone. He's wrong; but that's irrelevant.

"Where can we watch from?" I ask.

The elf leads us to a stand where his donations bucket is sitting. As he walks Clarissa onto the shooting grounds, he turns back and winks at me. Brennen empties the money from his pockets into the bucket. Halfway through, he thumbs a bill in his palm if he's trying to rip it one-handed. His eyes glisten. I resist the urge to turn around. I watch until he returns everything.

A rifle shot. Clarissa screams, then laughs, then screams.

Gina Challen

Undercurrents

She was glad to reach the towpath at the top of the embankment. Up here, the cold breeze stung her cheeks. It caught her hair and tugged it back from her face. She could see across the fields to the railway track, and beyond to the flash of vehicles on the bypass. She turned downriver, towards the distant coast, and for a moment thought she could taste the air, salty on her tongue.

That afternoon, she walked straight through town from the surgery, crossed the bridge, and decided to cut through the fields to the place where the river looped through the floodplain. The grey walls of Arundel Castle towered above her as she made her way down Mill Road. She shivered in the shadows.

Thin soled, her shoes were made for pavements, not for a track, rutted and littered with stones. She picked her way with care in case she twisted her ankle. How silly coming in this direction, but she hadn't felt up to bumping into people she knew and then exchanging pleasantries. Not yet. Not until she could answer in a steady voice, 'I'm good. How are you?'

The Arun was low. The tide was running out to the sea. She stared into the currents as they twisted through the broken bones of an old pontoon, and watched a plastic bottle spin in the eddies around the upright posts. The wind picked up, and brought the dank smell of mud from the exposed banks. Overhead, she heard the beat of wings, a pair of mute swans flew past, necks outstretched, and dropped into the river as if their bodies were too heavy to be held by the air. They circled, touched beak to beak, then they turned into the flow of the water. As she walked along the towpath, she followed them towards town.

As the days passed, it became easier not to leave the flat. She stopped going to the gym, stopped her late night swim sessions at the lido, and her weekly drinks with the girls. In the evenings, her voicemail buzzed constantly with friends wanting to catch up, an invite for supper, drinks. Her brother called his voice loud above the background noise of a pub. 'Hi Ruthie, how are you? I'll pop in later in the week, usual time. Let me know if it's a problem. We must sort out your fortieth.'

She listened to them all, and then sent brief text messages claiming the pressures of her job. She wanted to phone the office to plead a flu virus, but she wouldn't let anyone down. There were deadlines to meet, clients to deal with, and her staff to consider. It was the end of the tax year, her busiest time; she couldn't just stop, get into bed, and pull the duvet on top of her head. She told her secretary she was working from home. She started to smoke again.

She fell into a strange stasis, sitting at her laptop, not looking at spreadsheets, not making recommendations, or writing reports, instead she stared out of the window, her gaze drawn towards the river. Through the walls came the murmur of a television, a raised voice, and all the faint sounds of her neighbours. She thought about the swans swimming seaward with the tide.

One morning, she was surprised to find herself standing by the front door, keys clutched in her hand, her bare feet pushed into shoes, and her pyjamas under her coat.

That same day, around lunchtime, she smoked her last cigarette. How foolish she was to fall into the habit again after so many years. She would stop. But later, her need for nicotine consumed her, it forced her out of the flat and into the shops. Amongst the shoppers and tourists, she felt insubstantial, as if she were nothing more than her own jagged shadow. Once again, she fled the grey walls of the castle, passed over the bridge, down the steps onto the footpath, and hurried through the fields to the river, all the while hoping the swans would be there.

'Excuse me do you think you could help?'

Startled, she swung round to face him. She hadn't been aware of him until he spoke, and now he was so close beside her she felt he had been conjured from the ground. He was close enough for her to smell the woody spice of his aftershave. She stepped back. He was dressed in jeans and a dark coloured top.

'My daughter has gone missing. Please. Would you look at these photos? You may have seen her.'

She should speak, answer him, perhaps commiserate, but she couldn't find any words. Behind her the embankment sloped into the water, and across the floodplain, the bulk of the castle was stark against the hillside. The man held a small, rectangular photograph album. One photo per page. Handbag-size. She remembered her mother had one the same, and carried a much younger Ruth around, trapping her in perpetual childhood. He held the album against his chest, and flipped it open. Its red edges were bold against his black sweatshirt.

She looked at the photograph. A naked woman lay, spreadeagled on a bed, a man knelt beside her, erect penis in his hand. The colours were clear, and the detail was sharp. She could see the yellow shade on the lamp, could pick out the shine on the blue satin bedding. The pages turned. Picture replaced picture replaced picture. In each one they were posed ready for sex, on the bed, on the floor, on a sofa. And grinning, they were grinning. They looked straight at the lens and grinned at the camera.

Far-off on the by-pass, a car horn sounded.

Her heart pounded. Her cheeks burnt. Breathe, she

must breathe. She tried to swallow, but the back of her throat was dry. Shout. She should shout, push past him, and get away. The plastic sleeves covering the photos whispered against each other as he flicked through the album. It wasn't that time stood still, but that she had become immobile within it. The day was stuck, like the stylus on an old record, and she was caught, waiting for someone to lift the needle.

The pages stopped moving. He pushed his hand deep into his trouser pocket. She heard his quick shallow breaths. She stared at the photograph he held out. The woman was alone, sitting on the edge of the bed, her breasts full and round, the nipples dark jewels against her pale skin. Ruth was captivated. The album closed with a slap, and he tucked it inside his jacket. She raised her head. He was smiling at her, his eyes kind.

'Thank you for looking,' he said. And he stepped down from the embankment, and walked away along the footpath. When he was a dark, distant movement, she turned to follow the river back to town.

*

The letter from the hospital arrived. She placed it on the table with care, and smoothed it flat. Although the initial prognosis seemed frightening, she shouldn't feel scared, the doctor had reassured her in his surgery. The success rate was high. She was not alone.

'There are people to help you through this, Ruth.' When he'd patted her on the arm, his hand was heavy against her bones. 'And remember, we don't know for sure, at the moment.'

Easy to say, she'd thought. And there, as she stood in the hallway, she realised she should have asked the doctor why there was no pain at the moment. She should have explained that was the reason she hadn't seen him earlier. But what she should have done no longer mattered.

She decided she would tell her brother. Yet, before he was due, she tucked the letter back into the envelope, and pushed it to the bottom of her handbag, along with her cigarettes and lighter. When he arrived, she uncorked a bottle of her favourite red wine, and bickered gently with him about what food to order from the Indian takeaway on the corner. They ate, one at each end of the sofa, plates balanced on their knees. She listened while he talked of his work, of ending his current relationship, and of a holiday he might book.

'You're quiet,' he remarked, as he mopped round his plate with a piece of naan bread.

'Just tired,' she said, and smiled, nodding her head at the table where her laptop sat surrounded by files.

After he'd left, she cleared away, stacked the dishwasher, dropped the tinfoil containers into a bin liner, and rinsed the glasses. In the living room, the air was heady with the smell of onions and spices, and she unfastened the window. She wished she'd drunk more wine, wished she'd asked her brother to stay, wished he'd come back so they could sit up all night and talk. She wanted to call him. Instead, she lit a cigarette, and pulled a chair to the open window. Sounds carried up from the street, the click of heeled shoes on the pavement, snatched words, laughter, and the ring of a mobile. With her feet resting on the window sill, she watched the smoke from her cigarette curl into the darkness.

That night, she began to dream of the man. He had his back to her. She needed to see his face. It was important. She had questions to ask him. In the dream, she tried to recall his features by comparing him to the other men in her life. Did he look like her brother, her father, the doctor, work colleagues, old lovers? She was crying. It was as if the details of his face had fallen from her memory. She reached out, and touched his shoulder.

'Please turn round,' she said. She could see her hand resting against the black fabric of his sweatshirt.

She was jolted awake by his voice calling to her.

'Excuse me. Do you think you could help?'

A fingertip brushed her ribcage and as she pulled away, she realised it was a trickle of sweat running from between her breasts. The glow from the street lights crept around the edges of the curtains, outlining the furniture: wardrobe, chest of drawers in the chimney alcove, and her grandma's chair. Each piece loomed large in the gloom, as if it had stepped nearer to her, away from the walls. Before she could turn on the bedside lamp, images from the photographs spooled in front of her eyes. One after another, they jerked like the snatch of pictures in a third-rate home movie.

There was his voice, full of confidence. 'Make sure you look properly.'

Come morning, as she lay in her stale bedding, a sour stickiness on her skin, she was surprised to find she was alone. With her legs drawn up and her arms clamped around her breasts, she felt older than she thought it was possible to feel.

The dream began to seep into her daytime thoughts. She started to wonder about the people in the photographs. Who were they? Did they have children? Where did they live? Was this their real job? Was it how they paid the bills? Bought food? She thought about the woman's breasts. They were flawless. In her mind's eye, she pictured the woman pushing her fingers into the firmness of those perfect breasts. She imagined how the woman felt as the flesh surrendered to her touch, as she, this nameless, unknown woman, felt for an invisible, painless lump.

Always a whisper. 'Don't be scared.' It sounded like the doctor. It could have been the man.

She thought of other hands, strong and capable, with wiry dark hairs on the back of the thumb, the fingers pulling and probing her body, bruising her. She looked at her own hands, wrapped around a coffee mug; the skin was creased, the veins raised and blue. She couldn't believe they belonged to her.

*

On the day of her operation, she was up at dawn. She packed a bag, and left it in the hallway. Dropping her pyjamas on the floor, she stood naked in front of the mirror, and felt the weight of her breasts in her cupped hands. She dressed in loose clothes, and was comforted by the familiar soft cotton of her t-shirt, warm against her skin.

Outside, the early morning air was fresh and clean. She put the bag on the passenger seat of her car, locked the door, and began to walk, striding along, feeling the muscles in her calves pull against the pavement. The town was quiet. To her it felt peaceful as it waited for the hustle of the delivery lorries. At the crest of the bridge she paused and rested her arms on the parapet, her breasts pushed tight against the smooth stone.

The Arun was high. The undertow would be strong, grasping at the banks, dragging debris far upstream. She scratched her nails into the mortar, and a scrap of yellow lichen fell free, spiralling down to the water. She could see the empty towpath cutting through the flood plain, and curving away from the town. The breeze brought the whistle of the London train, the rumble of traffic, the bark of a dog, and the throb of beating wings. She lifted her face to the wind and saw the swans. Eight of them, necks outstretched, dashes of white against the blue sky, flying towards the river. She glanced down at her watch. It was time to go.

Olga Zilberbourg

Love and Hair

The stage crew had been drinking since *The Wizard of Oz Singalong* the night before and now the director, suffering from a sinus infection, was losing her voice, pleading over the phone with actors calling in sick. This was a radical departure from the spirit of fun and camaraderie I'd expected when I volunteered to perform in an amateur production of *The Vagina Monologues*. During our final run-through just hours before opening night curtain, we were three actors short and had to find substitutes. I'd recruited half a dozen of my friends to buy tickets—and what if any of them actually showed up? The lack of professionalism embarrassed me.

As the rehearsal finally got underway, my phone buzzed. The house manager turned to me and hissed, animal-like, "What's that?" She'd been getting on my nerves all afternoon, having berated me for bringing a burrito into the theatre and for daring to eat it while she talked to us about emergency exits. I ignored her and looked at my phone.

A text message: "I'm in San Francisco." My new phone failed to decode the number, but I had a good feeling the text came from this girl Hana, an Israeli who lived in Portland.

"Great," I texted back, "I'll see you after the show."

On the first night I'd met her, Hana put her hand on my shoulder, gripping firmly, and said, "You look so Russian, Yelena. I'd love to seduce you." Then she toasted me with whiskey and walked away. Hana provided a welcome relief from all the American women who wanted to talk about relationships as if they were a puzzle that required a Ph.D. to figure out. Hana didn't come to San Francisco often, but when she did we dared each other to do insane and ridiculous things, like hiking up to Twin Peaks in the middle of the night and dancing naked at the foot of Sutro Tower.

Daydreaming about Hana, I must've missed my cue, because now both the director and the house manager gesticulated at me like madwomen. I took my place center stage, and declaimed to the empty chairs my lines about the natural state of vaginas, good and hairy. I wasn't actress enough to enrich the lines with subtle degrees of emotion, but I could deliver the material plainly and effectively, speaking close enough to the microphone for all to hear. At just the right moment, I shook my head and let the pins fall out of my hair. It flowed down to my waist—a move I'd practiced in bars, usually targeting women out of my league. I walked off the stage convinced that I could bring the house down.

"Yelena, you've got to turn off your phone," the house manager whispered at me. "This is just rude."

I looked at my phone again, where a new message lit up: "Address please?" I texted the theatre's address and told Hana I'd meet her outside. I remembered her way of staring at me, a gaze she'd developed in the Israeli army to interrogate suspicious persons. Every time she gave me one of those looks, I felt ready to admit packing an AK-47 in my luggage. We hadn't slept together yet—not a matter of time and opportunity— Hana reveled in the flirtation as much as I enjoyed the anticipation. We teased each other and played up our strengths before a real relationship would necessarily expose our weaknesses. I planned to propose spending that night out on Ocean Beach, with no blankets or fire to keep us warm, only the heat of our breath—and maybe a bottle of vodka.

The house manager snuck up on me and tried to yank the phone from my hand. I held on tightly. "Go," she said, and pushed me toward the stage. I'd forgotten I had another small part to play in the interlude between two monologues. I walked on and delivered my lines, and, afterwards and for the rest of the run-through, hid at the back of the theatre, head buried in my script, trying to stay out of the house manager's sight. The rehearsal dragged on, with constant interruptions to adjust malfunctioning lights and microphones. The intern in the sound booth had his head in a bucket, puking out last night's booze. He bribed his little sister to help with the mixer, but now she fussed over him, failing to pay any attention to the action. The house manager tried very hard, but she lacked any kind of charisma or ability to organize people. I had no patience for uninteresting people. I needed to see Hana, the one person in the world to whom I could say, "I hate you," and expect to be kissed in return.

We were to rehearse bowing at the end of the play—the last time we tried it, one of the actors stepped on another's foot and tripped, dragging down the two women she'd been holding hands with. (I was at the end of the chain, and even so I'd almost fallen off the stage.) Because of the delays with people not showing up and the mic not functioning, the run-through ran exceedingly late, and there was only an hour left before curtain. I snuck outside, into the fresh air.

It was a chilly spring night, and the mist lay thick over San Francisco. A small crowd was forming at the entrance: *The Vagina Monologues* enthusiasts waiting to get inside. The show was sold out. In my brief involvement with this production, I'd met people who'd memorized all the scripted monologues, appearing in multiple performances each season, had crafted their own monologues, and traveled to festivals where Eve Ensler appeared in person. A whole geeky subculture had formed around this play, and I made a point of remaining an aloof outsider. I'd auditioned for the play to impress a date, and then the woman who had encouraged me to participate in the first place decided to move to Canada and wasn't even coming to the show. My life partner Minna and I were in the middle of a fight, and I couldn't reasonably expect her to come cheer me on. Personally, I thought the play was blah. It advocated for women's empowerment simplistically, without any kind of subtlety or emotional depth. Blame it on the Russian in me, but I wanted my art to be good and twisted, like life.

I loitered among the smokers, keeping a lookout for Hana. One of the men standing near the fire escape reminded me of someone I'd known in high school. He had trouble lighting a cigarette in the wind, and the way he lifted his collar and cupped his hands in front of his face was eerily familiar. The gesture belonged to a different time and place—Leningrad in the dark early 1990s. A sense of unreality enveloped me as I watched him pull out a cell phone from his pocket, look at it for a moment, then type something. He sent a message and put his phone away, and in an instant my phone vibrated in my pocket. I pulled out my phone and stared at it in disbelief. "I'm here," the message said.

At that moment the house manager must've given a go-ahead to open the doors, because the crowd started to move. My phone rang—the director, looking for me. The man who looked like Fedya puffed his cigarette and glanced at his watch. Last time I visited Moscow, a couple of years ago, Fedya told me he couldn't love me because he found my breasts intimidating and my head filled with silly American feminist ideas. Over the years, I'd heard other reasons: I lived too far away, I dragged him into the past, he was already married to my best friend. Best of all was his belief that I thought too much of him and so made it impossible for him to live up to my expectations.

If he were coming to America for even a short visit—the second of my classmates to cross the Atlantic—I should've heard about it. An unannounced arrival would be worse, it would imply an agenda, a let's-make-the-world-right kind of thing. The man turned his head and ran his hand through his hair in a gesture that seemed casual and yet intentional and self-conscious: Fedya. I made my way toward him through the crowd of enthused women. At that exact moment, his eyes fell on me and his face lit up in a smile. "Lenka," he said.

I found myself unable to speak. This scene seemed to have been born of my teenage daydreams, when I'd imagined Fedya walking toward me on a sundrenched beach, this exact look of happy recognition on his face. His skin under the yellow light of the theatre entrance looked unhealthy, and this sign of his—both of our—mortality washed over my heart in a wave of tenderness. Looking at Fedya was like looking at a part of myself I'd forgotten existed.

"Surprise!" Fedya made two steps toward me, but then stopped short of kissing me on the cheek or shaking hands. He looked into my eyes and grinned wider. His face wasn't conventionally handsome: his nose crooked, broken and his forehead slightly concave, but when he smiled his open, toothy smile, the individual features came together with a force of radiance and joy.

"Aren't you happy to see me?" Fedya asked in Russian.

"Fedya," I said, my mouth filled with his name, and all other words in my native language escaping me.

I could've shaken hands with him, hugged him California-style, or kissed him on the cheek in the

Russian manner, but instead I stood in front of him with my mouth open, unable to push any words out. I resisted the urge to reach out and touch him, but that only heightened the tension between us.

"Your phone's ringing," he said.

"Right. The show."

"Don't you work at the library? What's up with this theatre business? I've seen you try to act—you're not very good at it," he said.

"It's for charity, to end violence against women."

"What's this show, anyway? Some kind of strip-tease?"

"Oh shit." I hadn't the time or self-control to explain *The Vagina Monologues* to him. The play, I knew, had appeared on stages in Moscow and St. Petersburg, but that didn't mean that people like Fedya knew anything about the culture that created it. He would likely ridicule any explanation—feminism, according to him, was gender war started by women who didn't get enough sex. In a newer friend I would never have tolerated an ideology rooted in patriarchy, but Fedya's reactionary politics felt endearing. We'd survived our stormy adolescence together, an unbreakable bond.

I grabbed him by the sleeve of his jacket and headed for the service entrance. Inside, we bumped into a tall, fleshy woman whose body protruded from the straps of her black leather costume. Her name was Heather; she played the dominatrix on stage; by day, she worked as a kindergarten teacher. Heather had almost pulled out of the show with last minute stage jitters when she realized that the parents of two of her students might be in the audience. But then the director and the house manager talked girl power and managed to bring her back into the fold. Fedya whistled from behind my back.

"Yelena's here," Heather the dominatrix called out

into the theatre. She looked Fedya over and in her husky stage voice asked, "Who's your boy toy?" Perfectly in character, she reached out and with her long bright red fingernail scratched him on the cheek. Fedya was not a tall man, and she loomed over both of us as though we were children.

Fedya didn't miss a beat. He grabbed her hand, brought it down to his lips and planted a long and courteous kiss on the back of her hand.

"I like him," the dominatrix said, smiling at me. "The man's got manners."

He winked at her.

A fleeting thought entered my head about my high school friend who'd married Fedya all those years ago, and was still married to him despite Fedya's compulsive promiscuity. I pushed the memory away. I always suspected that he'd married her because I'd gone away to America; he took her because he was afraid to reach for me. Fedya's coming to me in San Francisco angered me on her behalf; at the same time, it upset me that she might think she had nothing to worry about: Lenka had her go at Fedya and couldn't make it stick. Not in a million years would she ever entertain the possibility that I no longer wanted him.

"Can we find a place for my friend?" I asked Heather.

"You have to ask the house manager, but she pretty much hates you right now. Where the hell did you go?"

I headed for the side entrance to the auditorium, but Fedya lingered behind, watching Heather even as I led him away. "Is she in the show?"

I pulled him through the door of the theatre. Some seats in front, I knew, had been reserved for friends of the cast. A few were still unoccupied, and I pushed Fedya into one of them, saying, "If anyone asks you to leave, pretend you don't speak English."

"All I'm saying," he said, "You stand no chance, next to that woman."

"And yet you love me."

I practically ran away from him and backstage bumped right into the house manager. "My friend just got here from Russia," I said.

"Makeup," she quietly screamed through clenched teeth. "Now!"

My costume consisted of a plain black skirt and a matching black turtleneck. I would enter the stage with a red scarf tied around my head, and after a few lines I'd unwrap it. The makeup artist—who, together with the lighting guy, were the closest things to professionals in this production—added paleness to my skin, deep shadows to my eyes, and made my lips look chapped. My character was a woman whose husband cheated on her and yet insisted that she shave her vagina to satisfy his desire. "You cannot love a vagina unless you love hair," my monologue began.

As the makeup artist helped me wrap the scarf around my head, I realized I'd be saying these words to Fedya in the front row. It was terrifying to think how much of the monologue applied to our relationship. Fedya had all but openly told me that perhaps he could love me if only I were a little bit less of myself: skinnier, flat-chested, considerably shorter than he, if I demurred to him not only in words but in spirit. "You always contradict me. And when you do say 'Yes,' I always feel you're humoring me," he'd said.

Fedya's wife—my friend—was much closer to the image of his ideal woman. She was the quietest person imaginable and had grown even quieter after their marriage. Whatever he asked of her, she did, from finding a second job to finance his start-up to, I imagined, what happened between them in bed. Yet whenever I talked to him he claimed to be unhappy. I wondered what had happened to make him want to change things, to finally seek me out.

The house manager hovered in the mirror behind my back, ready to guide me to the stage by the hand, if necessary. But I was ready. In my black outfit and white face under the red scarf I looked powerful and glamorous, a witch from Fedya's worst nightmare. The image gave me confidence. If Hana were here, she too couldn't help falling in love with me that night despite her crazy ideas about love. I was beautiful, and from the stage I could make them see this.

Following the cue, I marched onto the stage and easily launched into the monologue I'd had a painfully difficult time memorizing. I never once looked in Fedya's direction, not even to make sure that he didn't get booted out of the stolen seat. The husband in the story complained that the wife—I—didn't please him sexually, and the marital therapist took his side and advised me to let *him* shave my vagina. The husband reveled in shaving my vagina as if it were a being completely independent from me, as if it were the only thing of mine that he valued. I unraveled my scarf as I described the way he shaved me and the puffiness of my naked pubis. Finally, I had enough. Hair was there for a reason, I said. You can't pick and choose the parts you want. You have to make up your mind and take the whole package. And then I let the pins fall out of my hair and shook it out, aware of the way it glistened and shone in the spotlight. Then, I fixed Fedya with my gaze and told him that he had to accept me as I was. "Admit it," I said, "You'll never be happy without me."

There was some applause after that line, and I quickly retreated from the proscenium. The house manager didn't even look at me as she ushered the next actor past. The director pointed with her finger at the lines on the page in front of her: apparently, I'd gone off script. "Sorry," I mouthed to her. "Inspiration."

I'd never smoked in my life, but at that moment I craved a cigarette. I paced around the room, biting my fingernails, waiting for my next appearance on stage. I was over the whole thing. I remembered how excited I was for that one moment when I thought Hana would meet me after the show and we'd have our adventure. I shuddered at the incongruity of it. Did I really think I could escape that older, that insidious part of my psyche, conditioned to want a man and children and to be taken advantage of and submit, gladly? I longed for Hana, to share with her the brutally cold sunset over the Pacific Ocean, in my own neighborhood, and from there, to adventure down the rugged tracks, to test each other's limits. Ascend Half Dome. Hike the Sierras. We could stake out a camp in Death Valley, get lost in the American outback. That dream. But Hana stayed in Portland, and at this time of night was likely making love to some young punk. I felt the blind eyes of fate, hiding behind Fedya's weather-beaten visage, staring me down from the front row.

It took another hour for the play to finally end. By the time I'd rinsed off the makeup and put on my jeans and t-shirt, Fedya had escaped the theatre. I found him back on the street, in front of the front door, smoking.

"So," I said. "What did you think?"

"About what? The show? What did you want me to think?"

"I don't know! Did you like it? Was it boring? What did you think about what I said?"

"It was some kind of feminist thing, right? A bunch

of man-bashing?"

"Not exactly."

"Half of the performers seemed afraid of the microphone. You all looked terrified onstage. And what happened to the mic, anyway? It kept going in and out. I couldn't understand a word."

"Nothing? You understood nothing?"

"Still jetlagged," he said. "Kind of dozed off there in the middle."

Heather the dominatrix emerged from the theatre and approached us. She'd peeled off her costume, and now appeared in her plain kindergarten-teacher turtleneck. "A few of us are going out to a bar," she said. "Are you coming?"

"Sure," I said. At that moment Fedya placed his hand on my shoulder, on the naked skin next to my clavicle, and lightly massaged it. His breath, reeking of nicotine, tickled my skin.

"Fedya," I said in Russian, pulling away from him slightly, "We should celebrate with the troupe. You're not in a rush, are you?"

He smiled in response and patted my back. "I've come this far."

The bar was packed by the time we got there, with people spilled out into the sidewalk and the din of conversation audible from across the street. We squeezed inside, and Heather ordered a round of vodka shots in honor of our visiting Russian guest. Fedya toasted her in heavily accented English: "I have always heard that American women were ugly. Here's to breaking stereotypes!" He winked at me, indicating that his words were a put-on: Heather, without leather, looked pasty and overfed.

"Your friend is like a Neanderthal. Where did you

find him?" Heather said, moving away from Fedya. "It's charming at first, but then you get a sense that he means it."

I spotted both the house manager and the director deeper inside the bar. They were smiling and hugging everyone. They smiled and waved at me, too: now that the difficult part was over, all was forgiven, California-style, and they were ready to love me again. I introduced Fedya around and got us more drinks. Everyone was curious about the Russian visitor, and soon he was explaining that he was in San Francisco for a gaming conference, that he ran a company back in Moscow, and he hoped to open an office in Silicon Valley.

Somebody grabbed me by the forearm and demanded my attention. It was Minna, the woman I'd been living with for the past few years. Things weren't going well between us. I had little patience for all the "talks" and "relationship management" she seemed to think was necessary. Once, after a tedious week-long special collections cataloguing project, followed by a night of commiserating at a bar, I brought home and fucked my library co-worker that Minna knew to be married. The next day, Minna confronted me. Wasn't this the whole point of having a non-monogamous relationship, I argued. Weren't we free to sleep around without threatening our primary relationship? Minna asked about his wife. The sex wasn't the problem; the cheating was. That the wife hadn't been warned was a problem, Minna insisted. Each person had to be a voluntary participant in the open relationship, had the right to know all the parties involved. "You speak like a true scientist," I'd told her. "Nothing in life could be that clean." She took offence; perhaps I shouldn't have spoken so candidly. This episode was only the latest in a series of misunderstandings between us.

Splitting up in San Francisco had become nearly as difficult as in the Soviet Union of the 1980s. The rapidly rising rents far outpaced increases in wages, so if one of us had to move, she would likely have to say good-bye to the city. My name was on the lease, but I couldn't afford rent on my public library wages. Both of us hoped, I think, that things would blow over. I broke it off with the married man. Minna kept inviting me to happy hours to teach me ethics. I attended and apologized, again and again. Finally, she found some sort of a house-sitting gig with friends. I hadn't seen her in three weeks, during which time one of her plants died. "I'm sorry I couldn't make it to the show," Minna yelled over the noise of the general conversation.

"I didn't expect you to," I said. Even in the midst of a breakup, Minna apparently thought it her duty to be nice. She wore a tight velvet dress that she knew I loved peeling off her, and special occasion necklace and earrings. "Anyway, you didn't miss much."

"All that hair—let's see it!"

She pulled me closer and undid the pins holding my hair up. She was drunk, I could tell, and probably high. To Minna, weed and alcohol passed as acceptable forms of entertainment, while sex with a guy was off-limits simply because he'd once promised something and circumstances changed. This peculiarly Californian brand of prudishness struck me as humorous, but I decided not to bring it up. Fedya, behind me, made a noise of a horse clearing its nose. He moved my hair to the side, out of his face. Minna rolled her eyes—Men!—and spoke into my ear. "We need to talk."

"Minna, meet my old flame Fedya." I stepped aside so that they could see each other.

"He came all the way from Russia for this!" the house manager, triumphant, yelled from behind Fedya's shoulder, pushing another shot glass at him.

Minna put her arm around my shoulder, "I've missed you," she said, and leaned in to kiss me on the lips. I think she meant it earnestly. On any other day I would've reciprocated. Fedya's presence confused me. The kiss turned out to be an awkward and slobbery tongue-on-the corner of lip action. She'd had plenty of whiskey to mess her up.

I felt tired. I could appreciate how conflicted she must've been knowing that she still wanted me, despite her best judgment, but at the moment I felt like I couldn't handle the next round of talks and negotiations. I extricated myself from the embrace and explained, "Fedya and I are getting out of here. We've got to catch up."

Fedya stared at us with some curiosity, and I pushed past Minna and dragged him toward the door.

"Oooph," I said, as we were finally outside and on our own, instantly chilled by the fog. The rapidly descending cold scared the crowd off the street, and now we were alone under the muted light of the streetlamp. My hair was everywhere, and I shook it into place over my shoulders. I took Fedya's hand. He tilted his head and smiled. "What was that about? With that woman?"

"We used to date," I said, and quickly added, "But it hasn't worked out. Anyway, it doesn't matter now."

He raised his eyebrows and laughed. "You slept . . . you slept with a woman? How desperate are you?"

"Why, are you jealous? She's skinny, just the way you like them. And smart, too. She's a scientist, researching photosynthesis of algae. Probably too smart for you."

"I thought there was something wild about her."

I didn't like where this conversation was going—

clearly we needed to return to what mattered the most. "Fedya, don't you have something to tell me? What brings you here?"

And then he took a step forward, buried his hands in my hair and touched his lips to mine, pulling me in toward him. The fifteen-year old inside me squealed with delight. It wouldn't have mattered then that his breath stank of nicotine or that his touch was much too harsh and forceful; that the kiss was less about affection than a way for him to control the situation. For the sake of that fifteen-year old, I suppressed the initial revulsion and allowed myself to lap up the wonder of an unrealized dream. A few moments later, the fantasy grew too difficult to sustain and I pulled back the way I'd pulled back from Minna in the bar.

"So, you're into women now?" Fedya said, lighting up a cigarette and exhaling smoke into the misty air. "In a way, this explains a lot. I'm attracted to you, but when you behave like this—like a man—I lose the vibe. A woman's job is to be soft, agreeable."

"Fedya, I love you, but you can't keep saying this shit," I said. "People will think you're for real."

"I wish you weren't so aggressive," he said. "Why do you always need to push things?"

"Let's try this one last time, for old times' sake. Repeat after me. Lenka, I love you. I've crossed the ocean for you," I said. "We're too old to play games."

The door of the bar opened, releasing the blast of music and shouted conversation. Minna joined us out on the street, shivering despite her thick dress. "We've been together for half a decade," she said. "Can you seriously just walk away as though nothing had happened?"

"You left me," I reminded her. "I'm where I've always been. You're welcome to come back."

"Are you two actually a couple? What's this about?" Fedya asked in English, looking at Minna.

"Does he really need to be a part of this conversation? Look, Yelena, I'm really drunk and tired," Minna said. "I'm sorry I couldn't make it to the play. It's Friday night, nobody would cover my shift at the lab. I think your hair's beautiful, I think you're beautiful. You have a kind of energy that's unlike everyone I know."

"I've known you for twenty years," Fedya calculated, turning to me. "And now it turns out that you're a—a—Sapphist?"

"Seriously, who is this joker?"

"Minna, do you know this man here once told me my hair was best used for a mop?"

"My wife is . . . what's the word? She will have a baby," Fedya said. "A girl. It's being born next month. She's too . . . scared to talk about the baby. It's supposed to be secret. But I don't care about telling you," he said to Minna, "In English this doesn't matter."

"Congratulations to your wife," Minna said. "You should be by her side."

"I don't love her," he continued. "I'm thirty-six and I seem to myself an old man. Nobody asked me, did I want to have children. I came to San Francisco because of a conference, and I thought I'd surprise my old friend Lenka. And in return, what do I get? A different surprise!"

Minna looked pissed. "This isn't rocket science," she said. "If you didn't want to have a child, you should've used condoms. Even in Russia, they must know of condoms by now."

The thought of Hana occurred to me again. I imagined her as an arbiter, by my side, scanning this scene with lightning speed, and then turning to me: So, what seems to be the great difficulty here? Fuck conventional ethics, who needs it. This guy Fedya is a user and a whiner. He wouldn't stop at forcing you to shave your vagina, he would then ridicule you for the way it looks, pink and dumpy. Don't you think it's time to drop him like a sack of underinflated balls?

Once, when Fedya and I were fifteen, I stood in front of my literature class and recited a poem, my favorite. A love poem, it'd been censured in the Soviet Union and the author deemed a counter-revolutionary. The author had recently been rehabilitated by the Perestroika-era authorities, and yet my classmates and my teacher took issue with the poem. It confused them: why would a man tell his lover a story about a giraffe, roaming the shores of Lake Chad? What was so romantic about that? The poem had been rightly censured, they'd argued: It was a bad, meaningless poem. Fedya then came to my defense. Love, he said, has nothing to do with realism, but everything with the ability to picture an exquisite giraffe, whose coat, from a distance, looks like a colorful sail of a ship that might carry one across oceans to be with his beloved.

It's a beautiful memory, Hana would say. I'll give him credit, the man has imagination. But you do get that you've painted yourself as a giraffe in this scenario? Your long neck and flashy colors make you an easy target for the likes of Fedya. Congratulations: he caught you.

"I'm not asking anything that complicated, nothing beyond adherence to a set of basic rules," Minna began again, sidestepping Fedya and taking my hand.

"Minna, you cannot love a vagina unless you love hair," I said. "It's messy."

"You said that in the show, I recognize!" Fedya

said. "I thought it was silly. Women need men to survive."

"I've had time to think," Minna said. "I do care about you. I'm willing to let you get away with more than I could take from anyone else. I came here because . . ."

I stopped her and withdrew my hand. "Let's not do this now."

"It's nothing that complicated. Will you simply tell me that you love me too and that we have something . . ."

"You're tired, you're drunk. You'll be the first to regret this in the morning."

"Wait, let me—wait, are you actually breaking up with me?"

"That's pretty clear," Fedya piped in.

"I'm not kicking you out," I said. "I need a roommate to make rent."

"Don't tell me you're taking this clown home," Minna said. "Even you must have standards. On the other hand, I've never seen you say no to anyone."

"Fedya's an old friend." I strung my arm through his. "He's only here for what, a night? A weekend?"

"I'm leaving on Sunday."

"He's leaving on Sunday. We have a lot of catching up to do."

Minna could've made it easier on herself by walking away from me, returning to the bar or choosing a different bar, sprinkled like stars in this part of town, but she chose to play the part of the mortally wounded. "You're an asshole. That's it. You can fool most people, but really I don't think you have any idea what love is. And don't tell me about how the Soviet Union screwed with your head. I don't care. You've lived here long enough. Basic human emotions are simply beyond you."

The role suited her. Sombre, willowy in her shimmering dress, she braced herself with her arms, trying to ward off the cold, and looked on with disgust on her face as I led Fedya away toward my car.

I secured my hair in the usual bun on top of my head and drove Fedya to Twin Peaks, to the observation area I'd visited with Hana. The fog had thinned just enough for us to see the glow of lights downtown. We stood at the edge of the hill, side by side, shivering. Both of us were underdressed for the chilly night.

"You sure have come a long way from home. You've built this whole wacky life for yourself," Fedya said. "I don't approve, but, for what it's worth, I'm proud of you."

He stood next to me, close enough that I could touch him, but I would not. I accepted his words, my heart suddenly overflowing with gratitude to Fedya for showing up. "Do you remember? 'Far, far away from us, on Lake Chad, an exquisite giraffe roams.'"

"Gumilev? Yeah, of course, I know the poem. But why him, now? Lake Chad—aren't you mistaking the continents? Lake Chad's in Africa."

My phone buzzed: a library colleague, who'd missed the play, texting to ask how it went. Hana, I thought, with longing so powerful that I felt it as grains of sand in my mouth. I must go to Portland and find Hana.

Daniel Waugh

Last Call at the Rialto

It seemed to Juliet that time was never weighed more precisely than during these Wednesday afternoons, sitting silently in the great chamber. The steady, stoic incantation from the man on the dais separated one instant from the next more distinctly than the ticking of any clock, and held the assembled together in a great orchestrated hush.

The Three Js bent their heads dutifully along with two dozen other believers. As if held in a trance, their hands made small, scratching movements in time with the calling from on high.

Suddenly a strangled cry from the back of the chamber cracked the spell. To the accompaniment of a low rumble of voices from those assembled, the man on the dais confirmed what one hoped for and others feared.

The Three Js sat back in their seats as one, letting their felt-tip pens drop to the table and pushing away the papers that lay in front of them.

"I were that close," said Joan, the eldest – by three weeks – of the trio of women who met every Wednesday afternoon at the Rialto Bingo Club in Seacliff. "Bloomin' 21 again – that number never comes when you need it. Not in bingo, not in lottery, not in bloody life. Never when you need it."

"She's got the key to the door. Never been 21 before," Joan and Juliet chorused gently. The canon of well-worn jokes usually succeeded in lightening the momentary disappointment of not winning the house. Yet today there was no such relief. Today was different. Today the news had come that the Rialto was to close.

*

The Three Js had once been the Three JCs – but

that was back when Joyce Dooley was a Connolly and Juliet Smyth a Clitheroe. Born within six months of one another at the General Infirmary, they had met on the first day of their education at The Blessed Trinity. Later they would work together in Mr Hill's biscuit factory – an institution that for more than a century-and-a-half had given Seacliff a presence in the tea-rooms, front rooms and dining rooms of nation and empire.

Their first visits to the Rialto took place when it was still a picture house – queuing up outside to catch matinee performances on wet weekends and during school holidays. That was before hard times and a change in the law convinced the manager, Mr Smart, to bolster his takings by putting on games of bingo between the matinee and evening film screenings.

In a manner quite in keeping with her general outlook on life, old Mrs Connolly had chosen not to approve of the cinema manager's enterprise. Fearing for the moral corruption of her daughter, she forbade Joyce and her friends from visiting a place that she termed "that den of iniquity" (and in more colourful moments "Lucifer's Playhouse"). So the girls switched to the ABC in Ribsdale until the point – about a year later – that they felt bold enough to defy (so very covertly) Mrs Connolly's proscription.

The Rialto had always stood head and shoulders above the ABC or any of the other cinemas in the district. It was a true picture palace with its neo-gothic interior reputedly modelled on Pugin's Houses of Parliament – all rococo finials, oak panelling and Arthurian murals. A double staircase copied from the ballroom on the RMS Titanic swept customers from the foyer to the dress circle, where a brass plaque commemorated the cinema's opening by a now largely forgotten star of Vaudeville and various worthies from the Seacliff Corporation.

These days, slot machines crowded the foyer, creating a dazzling, cacophonous, disorientating maze for customers to navigate on the journey to the bingo stalls. The dress circle was now disused and while it still afforded spectacular views of the old cinema, it was rare that anyone troubled to visit it (let alone to dress for the occasion).

In truth, it wasn't even called the Rialto any more. One of the big national chains had taken it over more than a decade ago. The white neon sign that for more than 70 years had proudly proclaimed the Rialto's name – even penetrating the thick sea mists characteristic of this stretch of the coast – had been taken down shortly after the club's sale. The new owners had replaced the sign with a dull blue fibreglass awning which apologetically murmured the new name for the premises. Yet to the Three Js and most of the Wednesday afternoon crowd, it would always be the Rialto.

Only now, no-one was sure whether there would be a Rialto at all. Word had been circulating for a number of weeks that the club would be closed – and today the manager had confirmed the rumours.

"Ah well," said Joan as she started sweeping her things into what was (even for her) an extraordinarily large handbag, "it were on the cards. Place has been going downhill for years. Smokin' ban finally did for it, I reckon. Folk stopped comin' after that."

Joan was most commonly described as "a formidable woman". A stout lady of a certain age, she had a way of imposing herself on most situations in life. Considering herself something of a traditionalist, she tended to heavy woollens (often tweeds) and wore a headscarf to contain her coloured brown curls. Joyce was of similar build, but her dark hair was liberally shot through with white and showed fewer signs of care and attention. In fashion, Joyce sought to follow her friend's lead (not always successfully, in Joan's view); and the overall effect of her presentation conveyed significantly less force.

Juliet often thought that the pair of them (for she was rarely able to think on one without the other) resembled nothing so much as a pair of salt and pepper mills – solid, squat and complementary. Yet there were also times when the game-playing at the Rialto so animated their faces that Juliet could glimpse traces of the excitable girls in pig-tails who had befriended her a half a century earlier.

"Aye. I remember when you could hardly see from one side of hall to other, it were that smoky," Joyce recalled as she folded her reading glasses into their case and started to pack up her Wednesday charms. "There were lots of talk at the time about people packing in the ciggies but that were always daft. Lots of folk just stopped coming altogether. Just stayed home and smoked like."

As a child, Joyce had fallen in love with the superstition of the Mass and had at one time flirted with the idea of a vocation. In adulthood, her fascination had been slowly transferred from the church to a less defined spirituality. This in turn spawned a collection of relics, designed to attract good fortune. Her array of charms included (amongst other items) a lock of her grandson's hair enshrined in Perspex, a decaying rubber figure of Caspar the Friendly Ghost and a photograph of Elvis Presley; all of which were joined together on a "Welcome to Fabulous Las Vegas" key-ring that her son had brought back from a business trip in the days when he had been "on the up". She was convinced that these icons gave her the edge on Wednesday afternoons (and at other ad hoc occasions of more pressing need) and she would no more think of leaving the house without them than she would depart with no key.

"Well, perhaps it's all for the best," Juliet volunteered as they made their way back towards the foyer. "We've been saying for years now that we don't know why we bother coming so perhaps this is a chance to try something else."

Juliet was the baby of the trio, a softly spoken and slight woman who contrasted with the sturdier figures and more ebullient postures of her friends. Her watery blue eyes still contained the nervousness and hope of youth but her auburn hair had long ago faded to grey.

Juliet was the only one of the three to have attended university and later, when she returned to Seacliff, a job had been found for her in the factory's personnel department rather than on the production line. These developments had created a slight but permanent distance between her and her two pals.

"Aye, perhaps you're right," agreed Joan. "No doubt we should have stopped comin' long ago but…" she let her words trail off, choosing not to follow them to their logical conclusion. It seemed the easier course.

"Aye then. See you next week then," Joyce said as she and Joan turned in the direction of the bus stop, adding "Keep well!" over her shoulder.

"Keep well," Juliet echoed after her friends.

*

"Who's lad in suit?" asked Joyce one week later, looking towards the door to the foyer where the manager was talking, bending and apparently preparing to scrape to a tall man in blue pin-stripe worsted with thick black hair and nervous hands.

"Local MP – come to 'ave a look around while club's still here," replied Joan, turning in her seat to get a better look. "And while we're still around an' all an' able to put cross on ballot paper."

"I thought our MP was old Spooner."

"It wor but he 'ad to go when they found out about him fiddlin' with his expense account. New fella's not from round 'ere. He came up from London last year. Must've been desperate to become a politician."

"My but don't he look young?"

"Ah swear, country's being run by kids these days. Folk who don't know owt about real life. Wonder what he's doin' here."

"He's going to try to save our club; save our bingo," Juliet said, establishing a foothold in the conversation.

"Save our bingo? He might as well try to save me virginity for all good it'll do," Joan cackled as she tracked the young man's progress through the hall. "Any road, he'll do well to stay away from me. I'll have nowt to do with bloody politicians. Look at him – shaking 'ands with everyone. I'd be checking I still had all me rings and five fingers too if he tried that wi' me."

"Don't worry. Mrs Walsh is talking to him. He'll never get away from her," Juliet muttered as the Honourable Member moved off towards the stage and away from their table.

"Caroline Walsh? What's it got to do with 'er? She only started comin' here when they shut down Coronet – and we've hardly seen her this last six month. I reckon she only came today on account of bloomin' politician. She were always sucking up to teachers and sisters at school," said Joan. "Now if he really wants to know what's what, he should come and talk to me. I'd tell him truth – reason club is closing is because they 'aven't been looking after customers properly – not this rubbish about smoking and financial comics."

Juliet allowed herself a brief smile. She had been telling her pals about an item on the radio the day before on the 'national bingo crisis' (it seemed that pretty much everything on the radio these days was a 'crisis' of some sort or another) which she had caught while waiting for 'The Archers' to begin. The presenter had interviewed the chairman of the big company who owned the Rialto and a hundred or more similar establishments. He had explained that they were being forced to close clubs due to "changing demographics", "falling shareholder returns" and "the macro-economic situation"; language which Juliet had struggled to reconcile with her life and her club.

"Oh look. He's comin' over here now. He'll probably try to cosy up to us but I'll not speak to him," said Joan, puffing herself up so as to demand attention.

"I heard that a group of oldies started up a petition to take to Prime Minister in London," said Joyce, oblivious to her friend's mounting agitation. "They went all the way to Downing Street but then police wouldn't let them through gates. In the end, Prime Minister came out and invited them in for tea and a chat anyhow."

"They should've asked me to go. I'd 'ave told 'im a thing or two. Mind you, not that I would have — better things to do than to go traipsing down to bloomin' London," Joan returned, now arcing her back to stay in view of the parliamentary party.

"It would be fun to see inside Downing Street," said Juliet, "I wonder what it's like."

"Anyway, I doubt that it will get them anywhere. Leastwise it won't save our club," said Joan, trampling over her friend's musing. "Shhh… he's comin' over. Now let me do talkin' girls…"

"Read that bit again," implored Joyce, leaning across her bingo books to where Joan sat on the other side of the table. Her friend needed little encouragement and raised her half-moon reading glasses from where they sat, suspended by a lanyard on her imposing chest.

"Dear Mrs Cunningham. I wanted to thank you for taking the time to visit me in my constituency office last week, following our meeting at the Metro Bingo club. Bingo plays an important role within the Seacliff community and I will be writing to the Minister to find out what more can be done to ensure the survival of your club and clubs like it across the country. Yours sincerely. David Brindle, MP for Seacliff and Ribsdale."

"And he spent nearly an hour with you?" Joyce asked, eyeing the single sheet of bonded House of Commons paper as if it were some holy relic.

"Aye – and would have been longer too; but I had things to do – can't spend all day listening to politicians gassing on. Shook him up though – I think we'll see some action now."

"Well done Joan," said Juliet, even though she had misgivings about placing too much store by the words of any MP – even if the young man did seem awfully earnest. "Perhaps you ought to run for office yourself?"

"I might at that," said Joan, who seemed to give the matter greater consideration than her friend had intended before more pressing matters in the form of the next game of bingo imposed on her momentary political ambitions.

*

"They've only gone and bloody done it," said Juliet,

rushing up to her friends three months later. "They've cut the tax on bloody bingo and bloody beer!" She had been delayed getting to the club that Wednesday – an emergency visit to the supermarket for a disabled neighbour – and so had caught the news on the radio that the Chancellor of the Exchequer had halved the tax rate on bingo in his Budget statement.

Joan and Joyce looked up in astonishment – it wasn't often that they heard their friend swear – before the news started to sink in. From their table the news spread across the club. The excitement grew until something unprecedented happened – they stopped the bingo. Joan retrieved 'the letter' from her handbag and read it again for the umpteenth time as fellow 'Wednesday players' crowded around.

"So does this mean we're saved?" asked Joyce.

"Too right," said Joan. "When I put my mind to summat, you'd better watch out. Don't mind who you are – Member of bloomin' Parliament, Chancer of the Checkers, Prime Minister – you want to take notice when Joan Cunningham gets the bit between her teeth."

"This calls for a drink," said Juliet, gleefully breaking one of the unwritten rules of Wednesday bingo.

*

For Juliet, looking back on the two months that followed 'Bingo Day', life seemed particularly vivid. The reprieve had caused the friends to appreciate more keenly a companionship that, after so many years they had inevitably come to take for granted; yet the memories were bitter-sweet.

The sadness that she felt in retrospect was all the more poignant for its absence at the time; the happiness of those days was tinged in hindsight with a tragic quality of innocence. She felt the ache of a regret grounded in joy.

The first rumours that the Rialto was to close in spite of the tax cut were met with disbelief; and then with anger. Brandishing 'the letter', Joan swept into the manager's office, invoking everything from Magna Carta to the Battle of Britain in her demands that the club be kept open.

Juliet sensed that her friend's tirade would serve no good. She could see the futility of it all in the way that the young manager shrank back in his chair, visibly weighed down by fears for his own future.

Over the coming weeks, the initial talk of resistance gave way to resignation. Joan still carried 'the letter' in her handbag but it appeared less frequently than before and to less interest.

"You did your best; more than anyone else did," comforted Juliet.

"Aye – thanks J. I guess there's things in life that's beyond even the power of the Three Js", Joan breathed. "Ah well – eyes down, eh?"

*

Over the weeks, the Three Js would turn from time to time to the subject of what they would do with their Wednesdays once the club had closed for good. Alongside best intentions to put any money saved aside for feckless but treasured grandsons and nephews, the trio debated a long list of alternatives, from exercise classes to reading groups; ping pong at the community centre to Crown Green at the bowls club; baking cakes at the Women's Institute to the curry club at the local pub. In each instance, they failed to agree something that all were prepared to try. Nothing seemed moulded well enough to fit their collective needs – nothing so well as the bingo.

Far from helping with their predicament, the company that owned the bingo club seemed intent on persuading them to transfer their business to its bingo website. The main chamber of the hall was scattered with enticements to play bingo online but the ladies were unmoved.

"It isn't even real bingo," said Joyce. "I had a go once and the games were rubbish – and they kept sending me messages tryin' to get me to play the machine games instead."

"I 'eard that Dorothy Wood got into all kinds of bother, playing them games online," said Joan who possessed a keener ear than most for stories of human distress. "I 'eard she 'ad to sell house and move into a small flat on account of it all – and even that didn't learn her."

"This is what the world sees as progress now – everything and everyone goes online," said Juliet. "These companies will have us all living as hermits, locked away in our own homes, our bodies gone to fat and our brains just plugged into the telly."

"Ah J," said Joan. "You always were a daft one – for all of your university education. Ah reckon it must be from when we dropped you from slide in playground when we were little."

"So how do I play this mobile bingo game?" asked Joyce, who had been reading the marketing literature intently but with little in the way of enlightenment.

"Start by buying yerself a bloomin' mobile phone."

*

No-one knew what was likely to become of the Rialto. After all, nobody bought bingo clubs these days. Joyce had read an article in the newspaper about how African Christian spiritualist movements had converted a number of listed art deco cinemas and bingo clubs in London into churches. She speculated that the same might happen in Seacliff until Joan intervened: "Don't be daft. There's precious little spirit here in Seacliff and no bloody Africans."

*

It was a quirk of her character that Joan was rarely happier than when appalled with the behaviour of others. Her Wednesday afternoons at the Rialto gave her a chance to share her dismay at the ways of the world with her two childhood friends.

"Did you 'ear what 'appened over at Empire in Sandstones? Lady has 'eart attack during game of bingo. They call paramedics, ambulance and all – but then just carry on as though nowt 'as 'appened. I 'ear they's doin' resuscitation on the floor of the club while numbers is being called."

"I heard that too." Joyce corroborated, staking her claim in the story "I also heard someone pinched the poor woman's tickets, played 'em and claimed her prize when she won – and that's not right."

"I do like this place. But I shouldn't like to take my last breath here," said Juliet, sniffing the air as if to test the idea. Never someone who had felt particularly scandalised about life, she often found it a struggle to engage meaningfully with the club gossip.

*

The wind blew and the rain fell heavily on that last night at the Rialto but people came in their droves anyway. By 6.30pm, the queue had stretched out of the door, under umbrellas and around the corner into the car park, just as in the long gone days when 500 or more schoolchildren would line up impatiently to get in for the Saturday matinee with Audie Murphy, Randolph Scott or Jimmy Stewart.

About a hundred people took up seats in the old circle, some out of curiosity; most through necessity. From up there, the stalls appeared to seethe with bingo players, packed into the serried ranks of tables, with barely a seat spare in the house. Customers who hadn't been to the club in years showed up to lament its passing, perhaps regretting that the choice not to go to the bingo would no longer be theirs.

The 'Three Js' had agreed that they would not go on this final night. Emphatically they would not attend the Rialto's wake. After all, Wednesday and not Thursday was their bingo day; and it had been a while since they'd played evening sessions (not since Mr Dooley had passed four years earlier). Indeed they most certainly should not go, Joan had pronounced; but that hadn't stopped her calling up her friends in the morning to ask what time they should meet: "I 'ear it's going to be a sell-out and we don't want strangers taking our seats now."

A reporter and photographer from the local newspaper turned up to record the old club's passing, which added greatly to the group's excitement: "He won't be taking our pictures, I'll tell you that much," said Joan, "though it would only be fitting seeing as how we've been best customers."

It was the last of the great Rialto nights. The club had invited back an old time favourite to call the bingo.

The bar – normally so quiet – almost ran dry. The games span by in a whirl with each winner feted with cheers and the occasional burst of song. After the bingo had finished, some of the customers mounted the stage and the staff members joined in the drinking and the singing.

There were tears as well as song. Many of the employees had worked at the club since leaving school. It wouldn't be easy to find new jobs and certainly nothing like they had known.

The Three Js were not the last to leave. They would have liked to share a quiet moment with the club before the doors closed, but the carousing had reminded them why they were Wednesday afternoon players; and for Joan and Joyce there was a bus to catch.

Joan was uncharacteristically quiet as they made their way for the last time out through the club's doors and down the steps to the seafront. Turning away from the strand, she placed her hand on Juliet's slender wrist: "See you next week, love. Keep well."

*

A few days later, the builders moved in to administer the last rites, hammering chipboard into place on the doors and windows. The fibreglass awning was removed, revealing the ironwork which had supported the old Rialto sign. A faded mural advising passers-by that Lyon's Maid ice cream ("The ice cream everyone enjoys") was on sale in the foyer was also uncovered and a local historian turned up to photograph these hieroglyphics.

There were a few articles in the paper, speculating on the future of the building, and a number of enthusiastic citizens campaigned to set up a restoration fund; but most people had enough trouble of their own.

From time to time, Juliet would pass by the club and determine to get back in touch with her old pals. Sometimes it happened but more commonly it did not. Life simply got in the way.

The final meeting of the Three Js took place around a year later. Joan hadn't been well but news of the fire had prompted the three to meet in a café in the high street before walking down to the seafront to survey the damage.

The old picture house had been gutted by the blaze; its neo-gothic intricacies reduced to ashes and its images of Camelot to memories that had already begun their own process of decay. The three childhood friends stood holding hands, outside the wire fence erected by the fire brigade to protect trespassers from their own folly.

*

Three weeks later, Joyce climbed into Juliet's car for the short drive out to the headland across the bay from the town. The heavy fog and the vehicle's cramped interior seemed to suppress conversation that morning, the friends sharing barely a dozen words on their way out to the Blessed Trinity.

They sat silently, side by side, gloved hand in gloved hand, heads bowed through the memorial service as the man in the surplice intoned from the altar.

On bended knee, Juliet recalled a day of white lace and veils when the friends – in pre-figuration of future ceremonies – had first received the Body of Christ. This was the memory that she commended to her departing friend; the whispered orison of an awe-struck girl in pigtails.

After the service had finished and the cars had all departed, Juliet led Joyce across the churchyard. Passing through a gate in the drystone wall that retained the boundaries of the church they made their way to the clifftop. In a moment, the tranquillity of sacred ground seemed to have been replaced by the wonderful fury of nature as the waves seethed and spat on the rocks below.

Adjusting her gaze, Juliet looked out across the white-capped water at the seafront. There, towards the western end of the Promenade was the Rialto. The old place was just weeks away from demolition but that morning nature seemed to have restored it to full glory. Sea-mist veiled the fire damage and the morning sun sent brilliant shafts of light through the windows and doors of its art deco façade. Lost for a moment in her dream, she reached out her hand to Joyce and held tight.

Susan Haigh

Looking for Nathalie

I hadn't counted on Dani. For decades after I left Paris – if 'left' is the right word for what happened there – I was unable, unwilling, to recall a single detail of those delicate features; even now, I remember the shining beauty and flawless skin as if I were looking at a painting in an art gallery – captivating, but remote. Anyway, I haven't slept – not in any way you'd really call sleep – for twenty years. At night, the chill of cold sweat runs down my back from my scalp, so that by dawn the sheets on my bed smell musty and damp. To be sure, my waking nightmares have gradually become less vivid, but the images have melded into my soul.

In the nineteen-sixties I was an indolent, half-hearted student, with the academic ambition of a hibernating sloth. I was desperate to complete my architectural studies in Edinburgh as rapidly and with as little effort as possible and start earning money, preferably playing saxophone in a jazz band. My nights were spent in the smoke-fug of city jazz dives and my mornings in bed in my student hall of residence. Lectures were pretty low down on my list of priorities, so when I was obliged to spend a term studying the eighteenth-century buildings in the Latin Quarter of Paris, I was less than enthusiastic. Paris was an interference, an irritation.

I arrived at the Gare St Lazare in a soul-shrinking gale, in a city which had only just begun to recover its equilibrium after the Second World War. My face was numb with exhaustion and apprehension. Somehow, I hadn't expected Paris to be as cold as Scotland. After two false starts, I managed to navigate my way across the Ile de la Cité to Montparnasse, lugging my portfolio, a cumbersome bag and my saxophone case up and down the filthy staircases and escalators of the Métro -

in those days a gusty labyrinth where a wind the shape of garlic sausage and Gitane cigarettes blew constantly, a stench which seemed to seep from the walls themselves.

My room was in a hostel in a narrow street off the rue Froidevaux, in the shadow of the walls of the Montparnasse Cemetery. The old *concierge* glared through the dusty window of her office as I opened a door set into the gateway and stepped into a small, sunless courtyard.

"*Nom*", she demanded, unsmiling.

"Er, I … sorry?"

She had looked at me with expressionless eyes and rummaged under her table, and produced a crumpled form which she waved in my direction.

"*Nom de famille, prénom, nationalité!*" she barked again.

I dropped my luggage awkwardly, trying to hold on to my saxophone case at the same time, and felt in the pocket of my jacket for a pen, but could produce only a used Métro ticket. Muttering fiercely, the *concierge* dived under her table again. Seconds later her head reappeared and she slammed a chewed black pencil down on the ledge by the window, then screwed up her eyes to peer at a big clock on the wall. I followed her gaze – it was ten to eight. From the way she was staring at them, the green copper fingers might have been counting the minutes to the Apocalypse. At that moment the pencil had rolled off the ledge onto the floor. I lunged to retrieve it and my head met the corner of the iron window-frame. A thunder-bolt of pain shot through my skull behind my left ear and I let out a noise somewhere between a scream and a yelp, clasping the side of my head, expecting blood, at least. Looking up, I caught a sardonic half-smile of pleasure lifting one corner of the thin mouth, as though the wrinkled skin of her upper lip had been snagged by a fish-hook.

The stairway was musty and airless. It had not been swept for days, possibly weeks, judging from the collection of litter piled up in the corners of the steps. Alone and disorientated – *dépaysée* – and still shivering with cold and exhaustion, I unlocked the door of my room. It was the usual grim, ill-furnished student box. I dumped my canvas bag and portfolio in the middle of the bare floor and leaned my saxophone carefully against the wall. A strong mushroomy smell, like long-closed cellars, caught my nostrils as I went over to the iron bedstead and inspected the mattress. It was badly stained and a deep canyon ran lengthways down the centre. I did not look forward to my first encounter with it.

Gazing disconsolately at this alien roomscape, shoulders hunched against the penetrating chill of the place, I pulled my coat around me and slumped onto the only seat, an upright dining chair, which, like everything else in that rat-hole, was fit only for the flea-market.

The lavatory, out on the stair, was the hole-in-the-ground flush-and-jump type - universal in those days, but to be found only in certain *arrondissements* of the capital today. On the Monday of my arrival, and on every Monday morning after that, a strong smell of *eau de javel* permeated the landing; by the following morning, it had degenerated into the usual thick fog of colonic-methane-mixed-with- menstrual- blood-and-faeces, common to all female-only residences. The lock on the lavatory door had long since detached itself and considerable acrobatic skill was required to keep a hand firmly pressed against it whilst performing bodily functions. At those times, I envied the male capacity to at least urinate standing up, as far removed as possible from that disgusting pit, which stank as if it had digested the decomposed contents of the bowels of the whole of Paris.

Whenever I make my yearly pilgrimage to Paris now - a long attempt to close a deal with my conscience – it is to a city which has more or less lost the stench that characterizes my memories. Only sometimes, walking down a street in some distant *arrondissement,* do I catch a whiff of the old place, still there, hidden somewhere beneath the pavements. I pass an old man smoking a Gitane in the street - not in bars or clubs now - it's no longer allowed in the new smoke-free Europe; or I go into a house of a friend, inherited from a grandmother, and there it is – the ancient smell of France. All those emotions from the beginning of it come back, undiminished. I drink wine to wipe them from my memory, to take control of the past, but they always slip in through the gate before I can even give them a name.

The *propriétrice* of the establishment didn't present herself in person at any time during my stay in Montparnasse. Instead, she would leave messages with the *concierge,* who watched my comings and goings with sour suspicion, looking me up and down as if she were a sergeant-major inspecting a new recruit. Sometimes a finger would be lifted to halt my progress, then she would address me loudly with the hauteur of a countess fallen on hard times – which, it occurred me, she might have been. She always began her pronouncements with the same phrase:

"Madame a dit," followed by a tirade, the meaning of which inevitably escaped me.

When she saw that I had failed dismally to understand her instructions, she would repeat '*Madame's*' message, this time upping the volume by several decibels. Then she would make *tut-tutting* sounds with her tongue and wave her hands around in the air above her head, just as she had done at our first meeting. This I took to be an indication that I was being dismissed to the creaking staircase behind her little office.

I was in no hurry to report to my tutor in the rue de Grenelle and wasted the blustery April afternoons hanging round the sandy paths of the Montparnasse cemetery, gazing at the gravestones – the inscriptions told me they were poets, encyclopaedists, politicians, philosophers, mathematicians, but at that time I had never heard of them. I'd spend hours sitting on a particular bench - under the lime trees to avoid the worst of the cold rain – attempting to read *On The Road*; but whenever my eyes tried to follow the words, my mind would slip off the page onto some other more mundane subject – like how I was going to get through the next four months, having little money and no useable French; and how I was going to cope with the gutchurning horrors of the Parisian sewage system.

Sometimes, to comfort myself, I played my saxophone in the graveyard – I reckoned the dead wouldn't hear me anyway – or, if they did, it wouldn't bother them. On the third occasion, the *gardien* appeared, shouting at me from the other end of the alley, his peaked cap and uniform comically incongruous amongst my silent audience. It was obvious from his wild gestures that the gist of his tirade was as follows: *'If you don't take that damned thing out of my graveyard in the next two seconds, I'll ram it so far down your effing throat that you'll be blowing it through your arsehole.'*

Lately, I've been taking a more affluent, knowing approach to my little pilgrimages to that same cemetery. Now, I take a taxi to the gates, in the boulevard Edgar Guinet. I take my time over my visitations to the dead, pausing at the tomb of Jean-Paul Sartre and Simone de Beauvoir – a bizarre terminus for two life-times spent resisting the constraints of permanent relationship. I make a brief *salut* to Serge Gainsbourg, forever drowning in the flowers and toys and Metro tickets of the faithful; I look up my old friend, the enigmatic 'Riccardo', the seven-foot tall mosaic cat; then Samuel Beckett's dark, flat slate. Last of all, there's Alexandr Dreyfus, almost hidden from view by trailing honeysuckle these days, right at the back, near the wall. Not among the powerful and the famous, but in a secret, hardly-visited place. I found him by accident, years ago, just as I'd found Dani Benoist by accident. I'm the only one who goes there now, judging from the state of the plot. At one time, when I first came, there were the anniversary stones and flowers - stiff bouquets wrapped in coloured paper - and the ground was cleaned up – his parents, perhaps.

For a while I sit on a bench, the same one from long ago, under the limes, and struggle to imagine the young woman who used to try and read there, sheltering from the rain, hiding from the uncomfortable sophistication of these streets. Where is she now? I don't know. I might just as well be looking for the ghost of a stranger.

In the rue Fermat, I often went to bed hugging my

saxophone close to me like a lover. Sometimes I held it to my lips, playing quietly as I lay on my back, staring at the long cracks in the ceiling.

Three or four weeks into my stay, I was already asleep in the bottom of the damp canyon when there was a hammering at my door. I peered at my watch - it was after midnight. Thinking there must be an emergency - a fire or an accident - I struggled to my feet and out into the corridor. A tiny person, so childlike that it was impossible at first to tell whether it was male or female, was standing in the gloom of the hall; it was dressed in black from head to foot.

'Hello', it said in French. 'Who are you?'

The directness of the question took me by surprise - I would later understand that, had this same question been put to a member of a nation unwilling to part voluntarily with the even most insignificant piece of personal information, it would have been met with an icy glare. In France, such a delicate matter as a name is approached obliquely, if at all.

I held out my hand.

'Rose Baird.'

'Lose Beld?'

'Rrrose.'

I emphasised the 'R'. The tiny person repeated after me.

'*Lllose. Que tu fais là?*'

'*Je suis étudiante. Architecture.*'

I was irrationally pleased with myself at being able to communicate thus far with the homunculus. The fact that its language skills were clearly as rudimentary as my own gave me the confidence to continue.

'*Toi?*'

'Liang.'

'*Etudiant?*'

The response was delivered in unexpectedly rapid French, heavily accented and without recognisable grammatical structure, so that even the most fluent speaker might have had difficulty in following. My ear had managed to tune in to a single phrase - *femme de ménage*. She was a cleaner. She was female. I nodded enthusiastically.

At no point during her speech did Liang smile. I wondered why she had come to visit me at this hour. At the same time I was uncomfortably aware that she was staring past me at me the interior of my room, as if she were filling in time whilst waiting for a reaction to her diatribe.

Eventually, she sighed and made an irritated cradling movement with her arms. Then she held her hands against her face, palms together, and tilted her head to one side.

'Pas bruit, s'il te plaît. Bébé.'

Now I understood. She had a child. She'd been disturbed by my playing.

'Ah ,oui … er, non. Pas bruit.' I replied.

'Au'voir,' she said, solemnly, with a slight bow.

'Au revoir', I said, imitating without thinking the forward tilt of her upper body. For the first time, she smiled, showing two perfect rows of tiny, very white teeth. Then she turned and padded back up the stairs.

It was several days before I saw Liang again. I had detected none of the usual infant noises – no crying in the night, no shuffling, no calling. The place must surely have been empty. But I nevertheless gave up my night-time music sessions and was careful not to scrape my one chair across the bare floorboards.

When I did eventually see her again on the stairs, one evening after I had been to a small cinema I had discovered in a nearby street, I smiled at her encouragingly. Liang stared at me as if she had never seen me before.

When the opportunity arose, I asked Maria, an Italian student who lived on my floor, about my upstairs neighbour. I had spoken to Maria once or twice; hello, goodbye, that sort of thing - nothing more. She told me she had lived there for about three years and that she was from Naples. Maria seemed to know everyone in the hostel.

'*Liang! Ha! Bambino! Ha! Mama mia!*'

She threw her head back and laughed, showing her large white teeth, her arms flung wide.

'Liang, she's lying. She always lies. No baby. Liang is a *putain*.' She emphasised the word with a dismissive toss of her chin.

'She is frightened police are watching her. She think you are spying. They send her back – or to prison. She always does this with new people in this house.'

I must have looked blank, because she patted me on the arm apologetically.

'Men! She only has men, no baby. I don't like.' Maria's wide mouth turned down at the corners in an upside-down crescent.

Liang didn't speak to me again, but, sometimes, I would catch sight of her standing at her window, as I was walking back, and sometimes watching me from the landing of the floor above mine. At first, I assumed that she must have guessed that Maria had told me the truth, and that she was too ashamed to face me. I was wrong on both counts. Coming back late one night from a visit to Mhairi, a fellow Scot who had a room in Les Lilas – at that time an odd, run-down area in the east of the city - I had arrived at my door more than slightly drunk, thanks to the litre or so of wine she and I had consumed between us. Rummaging in my bag for my key, I leaned heavily against the door-frame. As I leaned, I felt the door itself give way and swing open. I guessed at once that the perpetrator of the devastation I found on the other side was Liang. She had been watching me, not out of embarrassment, nor out of fear, but so she could record my comings and goings. Instinctively I knew that it was she who had completely emptied my room, not just of my own possessions, but of everything except the iron bedstead and the curtains. My portfolio, my canvas bag and even a rackety fan had gone. The weirdest thing was that my saxophone was still standing, like a silent witness, in the corner. I remember panic boiling up in my chest as I rushed down the stairs – I can't imagine what purpose I had in my head – and out into the dark street. Somewhere in my subconscious I keep a faint memory-trace of a male voice shouting from what seems like a great distance. I had stumbled into the path of a taxi, then rolled away from the wheels and into the gutter.

Apart from a glancing blow to the head, which left me unconscious for hours, with two swollen black eyes and a three-week-long raging headache, the only other injury I had was a dislocated shoulder. When I emerged from a deep pit of unconsciousness in a Paris hospital - not from sleep, but from the emptiness of a brief coma - half - opening my eyes, I felt shards of late afternoon sunshine penetrate my brain. The sharp lime-green of horse-chestnut leaves reflected the light of a spring sky through a high window, streaking the walls of my room. Beside my bed, a carafe of water deflected the green-ness of the leaves onto the white sheets.

.

Turning my head painfully towards the light, I found myself staring at a stranger who was sitting beside me – I could see it was a man, or perhaps a boy. As I continued my upward spiral, I tried to bring the figure into focus. He stood up and I saw an indistinct outline and a blur of dark features and the glow of an orange kaftan shirt. The rest of him was invisible from where I lay. Leaning down towards my right ear, the young man spoke softly. I felt his breath on my skin, or, rather on the skin of the alien who had taken over my body.

'*Bonjour, mademoiselle.* I hope you are feeling better now. I have been waiting for you to wake up.' He spoke in heavily-accented English.

I closed my eyes again.

'Do you remember it, Rose?'

I rolled my head slowly back and forth across the pillow. I couldn't even remember which country I was in; all I could think about was the furious woodpecker trying to hammer its way out of my head via the base of my skull, just behind my left ear.

'Remember what?' I murmured.

Later, his words echoed loudly in my memory, as if they had come from the bottom of a lake, deep inside my gut, like bubbles escaping from mud.

'You were hit by a car – a taxi. You ran in front of him – he couldn't stop. And now you are in the Clinique St Michel. And I know that you are Rose - I found your name from your passport.'

'But I don't know you. Why are you here?'

The voice moved in closer. With each word a giant bell vibrated painfully in my head.

'I am here to look after you, Rose,' it whispered.

.

Dani Benoist, tall, elegant, his blue-black black curls tied in a purple headband, had been standing on the pavement as I burst out of the doorway of my *immeuble*. He had reached out a delicate brown hand to try to stop me, but I had stumbled on helplessly into the path of the taxi.

No-one had prevented Dani from climbing into the ambulance which took me to hospital. It was his impractical nature, together with a formidable capacity for infatuation, which eventually saved me from any possibility of ever becoming an architect.

Holding my fingers in his cool, narrow hand and stroking my hair, he said,

'Rose, I fell in love with you as soon as I saw you. Look at this beautiful hair – titian, I think you call it - and these green eyes – we never see such things in France. And you looked so helpless and lost when I found you, as if you had just arrived from another planet.'

'Planet Cheapo Plonk, you mean?' I said caustically.

'Cheapo plonk? What is this?'

'I mean I was drunk, Dani.'

Dani shook his head.

'In France we do not do this – get so drunk, I mean.'

I detected a note of reproach in his voice.

Dani visited me daily. No-one had ever fallen in love with me before; it felt strange and a little disorientating. I told him about the hostel and Liang. I told him about Scotland. By the time I left, he had persuaded me to move into his room in the rue Boulard.

We saw few people in those first days of our affair

and spent most of our time in bed. We talked – or rather Dani talked - endlessly – of Fidel and Che and the student unrest and we made love. He played the guitar and I played my saxophone, retrieved from the hostel. Dani confided in me that he was a member of a revolutionary faction called *Vie Nouvelle,* which planned, somehow, to bring down the de Gaulle government. Friends – Dani addressed them as *Comrade* - began to arrive in our room late at night. He introduced me as Nathalie, explaining that, even within the group, it was too dangerous to use real names. Talk of the New Society would go on until the early hours of the morning and joints were passed round. There were whispered huddles before they left, but still Dani explained nothing. Once, I'd caught sight of a passport half-hidden under the bed. As I bent down to pick it up, Dani had pushed roughly me out of the way and swept it up into his pocket.

I never saw my portfolio again, nor my canvas bag. I said nothing to my parents about Dani Benoist or about my Parisian exploits. Officially, I still lived in the student residence and my mail continued to be delivered to a *poste restante* in Montparnasse. Dani was my beautiful secret. Eleanor and James Baird had certain expectations of their children; their scheme did not involve boys like Dani. *Thrawn* was the word my mother always used to describe me. It meant I was unlikely to do anything she or anyone else told me to do - and was therefore bound to end up making an unforgivable mess of my life.

That year, the extraordinary intensity of the early

summer weather in Paris was unbearable for those forced, like us, to live in the claustrophobic, airless rooms on the top floors, opposite the setting sun, out of sight of the elegant apartments below. By July, the city was too oppressive for any kind of intimate physical human contact. Dani made up for the lack of sex by smoking more black than ever. At that time I rarely saw him without a roll-up between his lips.

In those days, the stench from the sewers and the drains became more and more pungent as the summer progressed, until the whole city was sweltering under a layer of noxious brown-stained fumes, made more nerve-wrenching by the endless roar of a constant stream of traffic and cascading sirens hurrying to other people's emergencies. That year, the roots of the *maronniers* in the wide boulevards had shrunk in the crumbling earth, their leaves burned up and their fruits shrivelled before they could ripen. Eventually, even the lime-trees stopped dripping, conserving their sap to avoid death.

We lived in a cramped *chambre de bonne* high above the streets of Montparnasse, opposite a little book-binder's shop and overlooking the cemetery. There was no heating and it cost almost nothing in the way of rent. The *concierge* - who was, if it were possible, even more acidic than her counterpart in the rue Fermat - would fix me with a wild stare whenever I came through the massive front door, which squeaked loudly on its hinges.

It was soon obvious that Dani didn't do any kind of paid work. He was a student leader – that was all I knew about him. He never spoke about his home or about his parents and whenever I asked him he would change the subject.

'Rose, you have to understand – I am an activist –

money is not my goal. I cannot work for money alone. If I am forced to do that, I cannot be *sérieux* – I cannot lead the revolution.

'Lobbing cobblestones at the *CRS* is one thing, Dany, but there's the rest of your life to think about.'

I heard myself sounding like my own mother.

I grew my hair and dyed it with henna. I had hardly any sense of the old Rose Baird any more – the shy child with frizzy red hair and glasses, standing at the academy gate, waiting for the bell to ring before she went in, so she wouldn't have to join in the inane conversations of her classmates. Now I stood outside pavement cafés in sandals and kaftan in the autumn rain and sold the Paris *Herald Tribune* and played my saxophone. Occasionally, a passer-by would drop a few coins into the open case. In the evenings I served vinegary wine and cheap brandy to customers at the Café des Sports, behind the Gare de Lyon. And later, in the night, Dani played his guitar and smoked pot until the early hours, whilst The Beatles sang *Hey Jude* and Françoise Hardy sang *Comment te dire adieu.*

'Jyorge Hérisson, he is a genius,' Dani would say, drawing deeply on a joint. 'One day, I will play like him. I will come with you to England and perhaps I will meet him. It is my dream.'

Afterwards, it wasn't Dani's perfect skin or his bones or his hair or the softness of his touch that I remembered (though they came back to me later), only my annoyance at his dogged insistence on referring to every country in the British Isles as England.

'It's Scotland, Dani, not England,' I repeated over and over again.

But then, I wasn't sure whether it was Dani or George I was in love with then – and it didn't seem to matter much.

In the afternoons, he would wait for the *comrades* as we lay in each other's arms. As a lover, I had nothing to compare him with, but he was gentle and, occasionally, when not too out of it with dope, passionate. What Dani lacked in modesty about his talents, he made up for by a touching unawareness of the extraordinary beauty of his body - his long, fine limbs, as fragile-looking as balsa-wood, narrow hips and high, rounded buttocks wouldn't have looked out of place on the androgynous fashion models of that era. His skin was uniformly brown, flawless and cool to my touch. Glossy ringlets hung over his shoulders and a line of fine black down grew along the outline of his top lip. My skin shivered and contracted into goosepimples as he kissed my hair, which was by now down to my shoulder-blades, and stroked my breasts with his long hands and kissed the insides of my arms and thighs. Afterwards, we would share a joint. He always seemed to end up smoking more of it than I did. The only aspect of his physical being which offended my sensibilities was his teeth, which were brown with nicotine. He seemed to be as untroubled by this as he was by the perfection of the rest of him. I suspect I would still find the youthful Dani as beautiful today as I did then, at the age of nineteen. Sometimes, I would lie on the mattress and study his features as he slept – this was always until mid-day – and try to imagine what sort of future we might have together.

From early in 1968, Dani began to talk incessantly of the rumblings of insurrection in the world – of Vietnam, the martyred Che and the hero Rudi

Dutschke, his life hanging by a thread; of King and Kennedy; of a Mexican massacre; of Tommie Smith's raised Olympic fist – a gesture which would cost him his career; of capitalism and Stalinism staggering on the verge of chaos; of Maoism on the lips of the young; of Romain Goupil's exclusion from the Lycée Condorcet. But most of all, he talked of Trotsky, Sartre and de Beauvoir, in one breath; and later he talked of Molotov Cocktails and someone called Daniel Cohn-Bendit.

One day in May, Dani came home and told me to get dressed and go down to the street with him. Things were happening in the capital – there was talk of civil war. I pulled on a coat over my thin dress and within minutes, we were in the Latin Quarter. Placards appeared, distributed by invisible hands. I heard the names Ché and Fidel as they passed from mouth to ear, but I still had little idea of what was happening. Nevertheless, I found my legs shaking and my mouth dry. Dani shouted to me that the students were supporting the Renault workers and that soon the whole country would be on strike.

Eventually, a small, tired-looking man with curly red hair appeared and climbed onto a wall. The crowd surged forward and I felt myself being forced into the centre of the melée. Cohn-Bendit's German accent – obvious even to me – floated out over the crowd. As he spoke he grew taller and his exhaustion turned into paralysing charisma. The crowd fell silent. I looked at Dani, who translated quietly in my ear.

'*The Revolutionary spirit is powerful within you - you do not need me to lead you. I have to tell you that I have been refused permission to stay here in Paris with you because of certain information that I have made freely available to the public. But I will follow the Movement from West Berlin. If you need me, you can call me.'*

The speaker raised a clenched fist and anticipation ran, shimmering like mercury amongst his followers.

The chant began slowly, somewhere in the heart of the crowd and rose to a crescendo; *"nous sommes tous des juifs allemands, nous sommes tous des juifs allemands."* We're all German Jews, German Jews, German Jews, German Jews.......

As the voices rose, the crowd began to surge forward, those in the front rows linking arms whilst the rest – thousands, all chanting now - were swept along behind. Dani reached out and grabbed my arm, forcing me into the mob, almost pulling me to my knees. He was talking urgently, but his words were lost in the din around us. I was forced to break into a trot to keep up with the growing stream of demonstrators. By the time we crossed the boulevard, squadrons of young people were joining the procession from left and right. Before we reached the corner of the rue Gay-Lussac I saw the first of the barricades – the street was blocked by great ramparts, a metre or more high - cobble stones, metal grills, uprooted tree-trunks, street signs torn from the pavements, overturned cars, all piled pele-mele into unbreachable fortresses; and on the other side of the barricade, rows of metal shields and steel helmets, goggles pushed up above the rims – Caesar's army waiting for the attack.

My aching muscles echoed the tension which loured in the air. Close to us, a childlike figure, its face obscured by a scarf, levered up cobble stones with an iron bar. Soon, dozens of others were following suit and stones were being passed down a chain of hands to those nearest the barricade. A hundred raised CRS batons were silhouetted against the lights on the far side like a gigantic Punch-and-Judy show. From a parapet high above the street a lone masked figure observed the scene.

Within minutes, armed reinforcements were leaping from rows of police vans. I tried to move aside as they closed ranks and charged the barricade, but the movement of the crowd propelled me forwards violently. Missiles flew over my head, landing on the other side of the barricade. Opaque clouds of gas followed the sharp crack of grenades and I felt tears burning channels into my face.

There was a deafening explosion as a car burst into flames. Sirens howled. Then smoke and fumes from the first Molotov cocktail filled the air and I turned to see where it had come from. I saw Dani hurtling towards me. As the bomb exploded, all noise seemed to be suspended for an instant, silence hanging trembling over the crowd; then a lanced boil of chairs, plates, ornaments, potatoes, tomatoes and bottles was raining down from the balconies, intended for the police, but landing on both sides of the barricade. Knives, table legs, buckets, petrol cans, lamps, were hurled from the shadows of upper floors. I crouched down and covered my head with my hands, protecting myself as best I could, creeping into a doorway.

Squad after squad of riot-armoured police was running towards us. Dani saw that I had ducked into the doorway and turned back, an angry, insistent scowl transforming his face. He grabbed my hand, pulling me roughly to my feet and towards the edge of the flow of the crowd.

'Come! Hurry! Now they start with batons,' he shouted in my face.

We were being swept along again; there was nowhere else to go. As I looked round, I saw a leather-gloved hand grab Dani's wrist. I looked up and saw an other hand holding a baton high above his head. I gasped as I felt urine running down the insides of my thighs. Somehow, I managed to kick the policeman somewhere between the balls and the hip. He staggered back for an instant, cursing and seeming to sway, both hands clasped to where my foot had targeted him. This time it was me dragging Dani by the hand down a narrow cobbled alleyway which led to the riverbank. Pausing for an instant to look round, we saw the heavily-built *flic* had recovered, his heavy boots pounding into the pavement. I struggled for breath, feeling my lungs about to explode.

Suddenly, we were at the water's edge. I saw Dani reach inside his jacket and pull something out. I thought it was another bomb, but now he was leaning back on his heels, panting, his arms tensed out straight in front of him. He seemed to be frozen, his narrow shoulders hunched, his eyes sighting along the barrel of a gun.

"*Arretez-vous, Alexandr Dreyfus*", shouted the policeman. "*Donnez-moi votre arme, ou je tire!*" Stop, hand over your gun or I shoot.

Confused, I looked at Dani and my throat contracted. My brain had stopped functioning, but Dani waved me sharply to one side as he continued to look steadily along the barrel, keeping the *flic* in his sights.

I saw a pistol glinting in the policeman's hand. The two men were poised, face-to-face in a silent stand-off, unmoving, close enough for each to smell the other's fear.

I think I shouted to Dani, but the sound that came out was drowned by the noise of blood in my ears. I tasted vomit on my lips.

There was an almost imperceptible twitch in Dani's

right shoulder and I realised he had squeezed the trigger back very gently. I think I must have shut my eyes, because I don't remember seeing him fire the gun, or the barrel flash which must have followed. I don't remember the noise it made, either. And it was years before I remembered the crumpled figure, its eyes looking directly into mine, before the armoured head crashed onto the kerbstone; then the torn blue uniform; then the blood pumping and pumping out, running along the gullies in between the cobblestones. For years, the only thing that stayed with me about that moment was the sound of the water lapping with inhuman gentleness against the embankment.

"Jump! jump!" I howled.

Dani seemed to hesitate, but I was pulling wildly at his coat, my fingers hooked into the button-holes.

I remember hearing the splash as I dragged him into the water with me; then I scrambled out on the opposite bank and ran, head down, close to the wall. At this distance, I no longer have any notion of time, but I think it was only minutes before I realised that I was alone; Dani must have got out further along the bank. Adrenalin drove me on; I ran and ran, not looking back, crossing the river further down until I was back in the rue Boulet. By some stroke of luck, if you can call it that, the *concierge* had left her grim office on some errand or other and didn't see the bedraggled, panting creature passing her window.

My hands were shaking so much that it took me several minutes of struggling with the key to open the door to our room. Once inside, I grabbed a rucksack and swept my clothes into it, dragging socks, under-wear, scarves, combs, passport and make-up from drawers, which I left upended on the floor. Within minutes, I'd ransacked the place. I took the rest of the money we had kept for food from a pot on the mantelpiece and stuffed it into my coat pocket.

It took me twelve or more hours to hitch-hike to Calais. I walked first to St Lazare, slowly, keeping to the streets well away from the Latin Quarter, to find the trains had stopped running, the drivers already striking. Setting out on foot, following the signs for the northern towns, it took five hours of walking in the dark, twice losing my way, before I got my first lift – there was little traffic on the road and I must have looked like a tramp after my recent soaking.

I felt uneasy as I pulled myself up into the cab of a lorry heading for Amsterdam. The driver looked at me sideways, then said,

'*Tu es vierge?*'

I didn't answer. Instead, I looked out of the window, my mind racing.

'*Pas grave,*' he said after a few minutes, shrugging his shoulders and handing me a plastic bottle of wine.

It smelled sharp, but I lifted it to my lips and drank deeply.

In the late eighties, I was working in New York. I remember flicking through the pages of an abandoned *Paris Match* in the faculty department staff-room – there was a piece on Jeanne Moreau and a bit on the British royals. At first I didn't take much notice of the faint black and white archive images on the next page, until I saw the title under the main shot.

Trotskyist activist Alexandr Dreyfus, known as Daniel

Benoist, instigator of a plot to assassinate de Gaulle, shoots policeman then drowns in Seine. Police are seeking his female accomplice, a foreigner thought to be using the nom de guerre 'Nathalie'.

The dark hair hung, limp and slightly out of focus, over the edge of the stretcher. I had to use a magnifying glass to be sure. It was him, all right. Dani's face was turned towards the camera, his eye closed.

Underneath, there was a photograph of a middle-aged man, strapped awkwardly into a wheelchair, the ribbon of the *Légion d'Honneur* in his lapel. Then there was the interview. The former CRS officer described in precise detail the moment in May 1968 which had ended his career, his marriage, devastated his parents; and he recalled how he had looked into my eyes seconds before I leaped into the Seine with Alexandr Dreyfus and how the police were still looking for 'Nathalie'.

Rob Hawke

All that Remains

Noelia is back. It's been a long time but the scars we share are not easily forgotten.

"*Amiga!*" I shout, walking out from the bar. "Someone's feeding you well!"

We embrace. There are streaks of grey in her hair. "You're not doing too bad yourself, Marcy!" she says, grabbing at my hips. She lets out that raucous, defiant laugh that makes me laugh too. The aura of the city is all over her. She takes a deep breath as if forcing herself to arrive.

Here in Calixto the air is heavy with the smell of razed fields and morning rain. The valley mists give a feeling of coolness and containment. All is calm bar the odd bash of a hammer or shriek of a rooster. Even the dogs are subdued.

I open up to make coffee.

"Long time, Noe!" I say, resting a mug beside her hammock.

"You're telling me! Who'd have thought we'd make it to thirty?" she grins, stretching out. "How's life in Calixto?"

"Fine, touch wood. Struggling on. My boy has just started primary. It's quiet, Noe, not like it was. The army hardly ever comes by here now."

"And the bar?"

"Business is ok. We're going to decorate. What do you think about green for the terrace?"

"Hang on a minute. *We* now is it?" I've heard about this new guy! Is he keeping you busy?"

Again the raucous laugh, a slap of her thigh. I've missed Noelia's insinuations. No one joshes me like that. We chatter on like old hens but I know she can't have come all this way on a social call.

"Marcy, listen," she says, straightening up. "I've been at Cuco's hearing. It started last week. We're involved with the prosecution. At the start he denied everything. But later they offered him a deal and he started talking."

"He confessed?"

She nods. "He thinks our husbands are buried outside Congoja."

"He *thinks?*"

"He says there's a grave near the quarry. He can't remember who they put there."

"Son of a bitch. How could anyone not remember that?"

Noelia shrugs, she's had to deal with too many Cucos. "They've ordered an exhumation next week, forensics, the whole deal. Some of the other widows will make the journey. I came to see if you'd come."

"Congoja is a long way. What if it's not them?"

Noelia's face falls stern. "Then we keep looking."

"I don't know," I say, still digesting the news. "It's a big deal after all this time. And things were just getting back to normal."

"I know it's upsetting," she says calmly, like a therapist. Noelia never sits still for long. "Listen, *amiga*, I have to organise a few things before it gets too hot. Take your time. And I might see you next week ok?"

"I'll think about it," I say.

She doesn't push. She knows that I'll think about nothing else.

It is ten years since Franklin was disappeared. October 20th 1998. No one bothers much with dates here; it's hill country, there are good harvests and bad harvests, years of flood and drought. The only other constant is war, sometimes close, sometimes like far off thunder. But 20th October I remember better than my own birthday. It is when life divided in two. Franklin and I had both just turned twenty. We'd been married a year and were planning a family. I know people tend just to remember the good bits but I swear I've never laughed as much as in those days. Franklin was a livewire, a new idea every day. He told me I kept his feet on the ground. I knew him so well, he said, that he trusted me more than he trusted himself. His latest dream was to build a ranch and herd buffalo, figuring that the taste of buffalo steak was so good it would make us rich. In order to save up we took over my uncle's bar. He'd given it to me before emigrating to Spain. He always said that for a poor person there was no kind of life here. But that's the older generation for you; they want nothing more than to pass on their worries. Running the bar came naturally to me. I'd grown up with six brothers so wasn't fazed by all the play-acting. It was hard work but not so hard that I didn't enjoy it. We even gave the place my name, *Marcy's Corner*. We gave it a lick of paint, a new dance floor, disco balls; our friends would come in and on weekends we'd stay dancing long after closing. The conflict was never far away, but at that time Calixto was more a place where they came to refuel than to fight. Sure, if a platoon or the rebels came in to the bar it put you on edge, but they usually just wanted a beer and to forget about things.

One morning while sweeping up I came across a list. There were twelve names printed in block capital, and below, a note: *ATTENTION RATS! You won't be helping the rebels when we bury you alive.* Franklin saw me freeze and ripped it up. His name was on the list but he refused to be intimidated. "A threat is only a threat," he said with a nervous smile. Others on the list didn't think so and took the next pick-up out of town.

A week later a gang of *Paras* came into the bar.

Everyone knew the *Paras* did the dirty work for the army. All night they sat drinking by themselves, not mixing, not dancing, just bringing a heavy atmosphere. When the bar was almost clear they called Franklin over. The leader was known as Cuco. He was two meters tall with dull green eyes. He wanted to know why we had let the rebels drink in our bar. "What else am I to do? If I don't serve them I'm screwed," Franklin replied. It wasn't the answer they wanted. They put a gun to his head and marched him outside. The rest of us were too terrified to move. That night, anyone who'd given the rebels so much as a cigarette was rounded up and marched into the darkness. I remember listening all night for a sound - a voice, a gunshot – but there was nothing. The next morning we counted that six men had been taken.

The feeling of panic was so intense that half of Calixto decided to leave. There must have been forty people crammed on each pick-up. Most of us went to the nearest city where we set up shelter in a hillside slum. The neighbourhood was crammed with shacks and open sewers, new *desplazados* arriving every day. But I hardly paid attention to the surroundings: finding Franklin was the only thing on my mind. We raised the alarm with the police, the district attorney, social support; long hours queuing in tall, cold buildings. All they would do was write down our statements. As the weeks went by it was clear the cases were gathering dust. Hearing my statement read back to me had felt like the defining moment of my life, yet soon I realised that no-one would ever bother to read it. "Don't be naïve," one officer told me when I returned to the station. "This isn't the story where the guy suddenly reappears. In this country, people who vanish end up in a shallow grave. Or they get chopped up and thrown in a river."

"It doesn't help," argued a woman behind me, "that the police never do anything to stop it." The voice belonged to Noelia, a woman from Calixto whose husband was also missing. I thought her big mouth was going to get us in trouble but the officer, weighing up the young, feisty *morena*, decided better of it.

The encounter with the officer destroyed any illusions I still harboured that anyone would help us find our husbands. It was time to face reality and I had two choices; stay and hustle in the city like a thousand other *desplazados*, or go back to Calixto. But looking back it wasn't really a choice. I needed to be close to Franklin. I needed to be there even if he came back in a box. Out of guilt, grief, duty, whatever you want to call it, I returned.

This is when Noelia and I became friends. Before then we had barely exchanged a word, but now our lives were entwined. Her husband, Tito, had been taken along with Franklin, his only sin being to let the rebels sleep in his outhouse. Tito didn't know it at the time but it was a death sentence. Along with me Noelia was the only other wife crazy enough to return. "Why should those bastards dictate what I do?" she said to anyone who questioned her wisdom. I worried about her toughness and envied it in equal measure. She was so full of rage and injustice, and had no idea what to do with it. I saw her blow up in the street at a soldier who tried to hit on her. That was Noelia, fighting on, not looking back.

I have never been that kind of person; intense feelings overwhelm me, there's no automatic impulse to fight back. My way is to weather the storm. Some call it passive, but I have always figured life will provide. Even so, I'd never had to deal with anything like this. I was incapable of returning to work, a friend helped with the bar, my confidence was in pieces. I was terrified to lay a memorial in case Cuco came after me. The *Paras* made regular patrols from their base nearby and had informants all over the town. I stopped going out, although truth be told I had little appetite for being seen. It was unnerving watching people freeze around me, to see their throats dry up not knowing what to say. Calixto became a very quiet place. At home I obsessed over menial tasks to avoid thinking. It was beyond me to touch Franklin's things or clear them away, moving them felt like betrayal. His clothes and records lay around me like in a museum. I had never understood all those war widows on TV banging on about finding the remains of their sons and husbands. What did it matter, I thought, raising all hell over a boxful of bones? Surely the memory of the person was the only thing that counted. I was wrong. It's the physical things, the T-shirts and letters. When your loved one is disappeared, the body becomes the most precious remnant of all.

It was a dark time and Noelia was the only one I could talk to. We were the same age but she was more streetwise, more like a big sister. She didn't ruminate in the same way but she could guess what I was going through. We'd sit quietly in the candlelight.

"It spooks me," I remember telling her. "It's as if Franklin is still here. I have... visions... of him entering the room. I know it's wrong but I let it play out; I act like it's real. Sometimes I wonder which one of us is the ghost."

"It's not your fault, Marcy. It's what they want: to chain us to our grief, to make us scared and submissive. But we have to move on with our lives."

"Moving on feels like giving up," I said, though I guessed she was right.

"Tito wouldn't have wanted me to fixate like that. I've put his things away. The only thing I keep is this photo." She held up a small black and white image of a young man with gravely determined eyes. "This is all I need. It tells me how Tito wanted the world to remember him. Dignity. That's what they could never take away. I think the same goes for Franklin."

I marvelled at how quickly she had been able to order things in her mind.

As time went on the *Paras* introduced a whole new trade to the town. No one bothered farming corn anymore, the fields were thick with coca bushes. It was simple economics; farmers could double what they made on food crops. For a while people thought they were getting a good deal, it was illegal but the army didn't seem to mind. They did a sweep now and then for the sake of appearances, but no-one was fooled; they were in it up to their eyeballs. Noelia came to see me one day. She'd started seeing a guy who worked in a forest lab cooking up coca base, a smart-mover they called Gato. Noelia had the look of someone in a hurry, determined not to miss any chance life threw up.

"Just think Marcy. He makes five times what the farmers do. If we did it for a couple of years that would be enough to move out for good. And not to some *barrio de desplazados* but to somewhere decent, anywhere we want."

"I'm not sure I have the nerve for that kind of life."

"You're smart Marcy, you would pick it up. I know it's a shit business but it's a means to an end. This is our ticket out."

I didn't disapprove, it's not as if there were any normal jobs. I gave it some thought, but my mind kept returning to Franklin and his dream of a buffalo ranch; the dream of following what he loved doing and what he was good at.

"Sorry, Noe," I said, "I think it's time I went back to running the bar."

I saw less of Noelia after that. Her new job meant taking precautions, and she wanted to keep me away from it. I later heard that she married Gato in secret and became his partner in crime. Her daring amazed me. Quietly, I began working shifts at the bar. It was good to pretend I was still the same person as before. Deafening, drunken nights of *vallenatos* almost pushed everything else out of my mind. But this idea of who I was then and who I was now was hard to reconcile. The loss of Franklin had made me two different people. People were kind in their way, although out of sensitivity or fear no one dared to mention what happened. It occurred to me that they simply wanted to forget. "Welcome to the land of amnesia," Noelia once told me, "forgetting is the safest way. They'll never admit it but what people most wish is for you to swallow your grief." I didn't apportion blame, but for me forgetting wasn't an option, the memory ran in my blood.

Strangers made me jumpy. Whenever the *Paras* came by I felt paralysed and couldn't breathe until they had gone. I lived in fear that Cuco himself would return. Perhaps inevitably I hooked up with the first guy that made me feel safe. He was three years my junior, a timber cutter, strong and tough. Of course, faced with a sub-automatic he would blink like anyone else, but his fearlessness, bred by inexperience, was enough to win me over. He didn't waste any time in making moves. Deep down I knew I wasn't ready but at the same time Noelia was right; it's no good getting stuck. After six months I married him. Big mistake. He was eaten by jealousy; unable to handle my grief he flew into a fury destroying Franklin's things and even banning mention of his name. When he finally moved out I was left with a two-month old baby.

Again, Noelia was there to help pick up the pieces. Although she only came into town once in a while, she sent money for utilities and baby clothes. "Anyone could have made the same mistake," she told me, "it's the only way to learn. You weren't to know." I didn't fully realise it at the time but Noelia's words could easily have been intended for herself. In spite of the extra income, her new life was not working as planned. When we met up she was tense and distracted. The word was that her new man Gato had overstepped himself with the *Paras*. Depending who you asked Gato was either a trouble maker putting everyone's business on the line, or a hero standing up for a fair deal. Noelia defended him, but she was fast learning that coca was more trouble than it was worth. No one was getting rich, no one was allowed to stop production; it amounted to little more than bonded labour.

The day came when Gato resisted too loudly and they put a bullet in his head. The truth was probably more nuanced, some say he was making deals on the side, but it didn't pay to ask too many questions. Either way it meant that there was no place left for Noelia in Calixto. It all happened in a blur. She was so nervous and het up there was no time to absorb the loss. Within days she had fled to the city to join the social movement. Two husbands was her limit; she was determined to do something about it. We still spoke on the phone, but from that moment our lives diverged.

The killing of Gato had shaken things up. The *Paras*, who'd taken a back seat, were now doing more regular patrols, as if to remind any doubters who was really calling the shots. But there was a sense of desperation to it, as if their control was ebbing. One or two soldiers asked me about Noelia but I always played dumb. With Noelia gone the feeling of exposure intensified; I was far from standing on my own two feet. I began to think maybe it was also time that I left. After the disaster with the logger I had put all thoughts of remarrying aside. All hopes I had were for my baby boy; I filled him with love and pledged that someday I'd give him a new life. A life where he wasn't tied on my back while I slung *aguardiente*. Although it was home it was hard to see much hope in Calixto. The *Paras* kept telling us life under them was simple; do this and do that and there's nothing to worry about. But they rarely stopped to warn you when the rules changed.

One day, I came back from picking up a box of *Frito Lays* from a commerce truck, and waiting in the bar was Cuco himself. I could never forget those dull green eyes. There were two men with him and they weren't stopping to drink.

"Are you going to tell me where Noelia is?" asked Cuco

"She went to live in the city. I don't know any more than that. I haven't heard from her."

"There's no point covering for her, she's up to no good."

Anger rose up through the fear. "I've no idea what she's up to. We don't speak anymore."

He laughed. "When you do speak to her, tell her I'm coming."

There was no doubt he knew I was lying. I felt my heart in my throat. "Cuco," I spoke up, as he turned to leave. "What happened to my husband?"

He grimaced. "He got what was coming to him. Enough stupid questions, ok?"

Who knows how but I stood my ground. "No. I

need more than that. What if it happened to you, to someone you love?"

He came close, his eyes full of torment. I thought he would hit me, or worse.

"It has," he said. "It has happened to me."

I never saw Cuco again after that. Times were changing. The real problem was that the army couldn't guarantee immunity for the *Paras* anymore. In an attempt to clean things up, the government sent in counter-narcotics troops to tear up and fumigate the coca. Like a game of cat and mouse, the farmers replanted, but the cat was winning. Seeing their profits dwindle, most of the *Paras* left, taking the coca trade with them. Calixto changed overnight. Some farmers returned to planting food crops, although with the damaged soil, low prices, and loss of knowhow, others chose to cut their losses and move to the city. Although the slump hit takings in the bar, I was less inclined to leave. The encounter with Cuco had rekindled a feeling of self-respect that had been lacking for so long. The time for hiding was over. I made a small shrine in the cemetery for Franklin and visited every day. If anyone removed it, I thought, I would just make another. This simple act gave so much relief that I didn't care about the kids who followed sniggering. *La vieja* they called me, the old woman. I had only just turned twenty-seven.

One day Noelia phoned from the city and as ever her life was steamrollering on. They had trained her up as a paralegal and she spent her days taking testimony and filing cases. She was in her element. She told me the news that Cuco had been caught, or rather he had handed himself in. Her voice was hard. "Justice," she said, almost in triumph. It was difficult to feel satisfaction. I felt that her idea of justice and mine were different.

Three more years would pass before Cuco actually saw a court room. I told myself to get on with life, not to hold my breath, but the truth is not a day went by when it didn't cross my mind. Meanwhile, the closure of a nearby bar gave a boost to Marcy's Corner, enough to take on extra help. I hired a guy called Abelardo who proved to be steady, reliable, and good company. He was ten years older than me and was also raising a kid on his own. It allowed me to take another job helping out at the primary school, the money from which I put in a college fund for my boy. It felt good to be making it on my own terms. I was even able to get Franklin a proper headstone. It had only taken ten years! It wasn't long before Abelardo fell in love with me. I told him straight up about Franklin, that I wouldn't stand for any jealousy. But he knew well enough, he had lost a son who had been conscripted and killed in the army. His tenderness and his way with the kids made me start to love him back. For the first time since Franklin there was someone with whom I could dream about the future.

*

The day Noelia arrives with the exhumation unit Abelardo is painting the bar bright green. We stop decorating to make everyone breakfast. There are anthropologists, forensic technicians, investigators; all starchy types from the capital who look completely out of place. There are also the widows and mothers of the other victims who I haven't seen in a decade. Two police officers are there to give us security. How times change. Half of the town has turned out to study the new arrivals; it's not every day a fleet of shiny Toyotas pulls into town.

"Are you ready?" Noelia asks pulling me aside after breakfast.

"I've had my bag ready all week."

The journey to Congoja is two days overland by foot. A pack of mules is assembled in the main square. At the last minute about a dozen extra people from town decide to join us, a gesture which warms my heart. I kiss Abelardo and my boy goodbye and set off at Noelia's side. To start with it is pleasant and everyone is full of life. You can see why the poets go on about the *campo*; the colours are so clear and bright. But soon the trail narrows and silence is the rule. There is hardly anyone in sight, just the odd farmer or muleteer. It's been years since I've walked this way, there were mines and God knows who you would run into. I can't help but imagine Franklin being marched down the trail. In my mind he is still a boy, it is disconcerting to think he would now be thirty.

The city types are an odd sight, slipping on their backsides. I stick close to Noelia, admiring how adept she has become, how worldly. At one moment she is chattering away about politics, the next she is holding my hand in silence. We reach Congoja on the second day. The houses are all leaking and there's no electricity; it makes Calixto look like a capital city. I look up a couple of old acquaintances but mostly people are wary of our incursion. An old woman selling bitter *limonada* warns that digging around will only stir up trouble. The night is tense; if anything were to happen here it would be days before anyone found out. Things are not like they were but you can't take anything for granted.

At dawn the exhumation is set up beside a grove of plantains. Even at 7am the heat makes the air tremble, the fruit hangs low and heavy. The instruments that have rattled along on mule-back are now unpacked and placed under a canvas shelter. I stare like a child at the strangeness of the procedure, like at surgeons preparing for an operation. Every step is registered on laptops and machines I have never seen before. Helping with the dig are some adolescents from the village, lean and simple kids happy to show their strength. I wonder how much they understand what is happening. We form a crescent around the trench in our plastic chairs. Some of the widows are already weeping. We watch in silence as the boys plough down into the earth. Noelia's grip hurts but I don't have the heart to tell her.

It isn't long before the sound of spade on bone is heard. The sharp scraping triggers a collective shudder. Bones are removed that could easily belong to a dog or a goat, but it is soon obvious that the remains are human. A pelvis, a hand, a skull; one by one they are passed along, photographed and logged. A man in smocks with long white gloves assembles the pieces like some morbid jigsaw. Unable to watch Noelia creases over onto my lap and begins to sob. Her grief is so strong that it shocks me more than the sight of the bones. After some hours the full skeletons of six bodies are recovered. There are no extra features; rings and watches have been stripped and the clothes are long since decayed. It will be a while before the DNA tests come back but six is the right number, and, you might call it hoodoo, but none of us has any doubt it's them. Surprisingly, the main sensation I feel is relief, comfort that Franklin will be coming home. I've never let him far from my sight, even when I worried it would drive me mad. The idea that they will now have to pack his remains off to the city for tests and reconstructions makes me consider doing irrational things not to lose sight of him again. But after all this time I know I can withstand a few more weeks.

As for Noelia, I have never seen her like this. Long after the dig is called to a close, after the other widows have sought shade in the village, she is still convulsing in my arms. Her eyes are elsewhere, full of pain and longing. I stroke her crown to sooth her but her sorrow is endless. Flies crawl up her arms; I'm not even sure she registers my voice. For all these years she has been the rock to whom others have clung, the one who has held me together. And now tightly I hold onto her, worried that she is the one who will break.

Notes on Contributors

Gina Challen is originally from London. She moved to West Sussex in 1979. In 2012, she left her job as an insurance broker to complete a masters degree in creative writing. This she fondly refers to as her mid-life crisis. Although originally a city girl, the farmsteads and woods of the downlands hold her heart, they are the inspiration for her writing, the landscape to which she knows she belongs. Previously, her stories have been anthologised in The Bristol Short Story Prize Volume 8 2015, the Cinnamon Press Short Story Award collections 2012 & 2013, and the Willesden Herald New Short Stories 8, 2014 and Rattle Tales 2, 2012. Two of her stories were shortlisted for the prestigious Bridport Prize in 2014. You can also find her stories and critical essays online with Ink Tears and Storgy magazines and Thresholds Short Story Forum. She is currently working on a short story collection.
www.ginachallen.co.uk

Tracy Fells lives close to the South Downs in glorious West Sussex. She has won awards for both fiction and drama. Her short stories have appeared in *Firewords Quarterly*, *The Yellow Room* and *Writer's Forum*, online at *Litro New York*, *Short Story Sunday* and in anthologies such as *Fugue*, *Rattle Tales* and *A Box of Stars Beneath the Bed*. Competition success includes short-listings for the Commonwealth Writers Short Story Prize, Brighton Prize, Fish Short Story and Flash Fiction Prizes. Tracy completed her MA in Creative Writing at Chichester

University in 2016 and is currently seeking represent-
ation for a crime mystery novel and her short story
collection. She shares a blog with The Literary Pig
(tracyfells.blogspot.co.uk) and tweets as @theliterarypig.

Susan Haigh returned to north-east Fife in 2013, having spent eight years living in a cave house in the Loire
Valley. She had previously worked on a series of short
stories, supported by a Scottish Book Trust mentoring
scheme, and continued to write stories and a novel in a
caravan under a vine by a river (not as glamorous as it
sounds!). Her work has won several awards in Britain
and the USA and has been published in *Mslexia, Cadenza*
Magazine, *Sunpenny* Anthology, *New Writing Dundee 8,
Beginning* Anthology, the Scottish Arts Club Short Story
Awards website, the *Women of Dundee and Books*
anthology and a number of American journals and
anthologies. In 2016 she appeared on a short list of six
for a Scottish Book Trust New Writers Award and
published poems in Scottish literary journals, *Northwords
Now, Gutter* Magazine and the StAnza Map of Scotland
in Poems. She was also a finalist in the 2016 Scottish
Arts Club Short Story Competition. She reviews and
interviews for a number of journals, including Dundee
University Review of the Arts. She teaches German at
Dundee University.

Rob Hawke lives and works in Camberwell, London.
His short fiction has featured in Momaya Short Story
Review and Shooter Literary Magazine, and he holds an
MA in Creative and Critical Writing from University of
Sussex. He is currently working on his first full length
novel, a political drama set in South West England. To
support his writing Rob works part time at a psychology
institute.

Anna Lewis's stories have appeared in journals including *New Welsh Review* and *The Interpreter's House*. Her stories and poems have won several awards, and she was short-listed for the Willesden Herald short story prize in 2013. She is the author of two poetry collections: *Other Harbours* (Parthian, 2012) and *The Blue Cell* (Rack Press, 2015). She lives in Cardiff.

David Lewis grew up in Oklahoma, did an MA at UCL in London and now lives in Paris. His short stories and essays have appeared in *J'aime mon quartier, je ramasse, Chelsea Station, Liars' League, The 2013 Fish Anthology, Indestructible* and *Talking Points Memo*. He irregularly posts essays and translations on Medium, as @dwlewis.

Catherine McNamara grew up in Sydney, ran away to Paris to write, and ended up in West Africa running a bar. She was an embassy secretary in pre-war Mogadishu, and has worked as an au pair, graphic designer, translator, English teacher and shoe model. Her short story collection *Pelt and Other Stories* was long-listed for the Frank O'Connor Award and semi-finalist in the Hudson Prize. Her work has been Pushcart-nominated and published in the U.K., Europe, U.S.A. and Australia. Catherine lives in Italy.

Barbara Robinson was born in Manchester where she still lives, writes and works. She writes short stories and is currently working on her first novel, Elbow Street.

Daniel Waugh was born in London and has lived in France and Yorkshire. He lives in Wimbledon with his wife, three-year-old daughter and black cat. 'Last Call at the Rialto' is his first short story.

Olga Zilberbourg grew up in St. Petersburg, Russia and moved to the United States at the age of seventeen. Her English-language fiction is forthcoming from World Literature Today, Feminist Studies, and California Prose Directory; stories have appeared in J Journal, Epiphany, Narrative Magazine, Printers Row, Hobart, Santa Monica Review, among others. She serves as a co-facilitator of the weekly San Francisco Writers Workshop.